Apted PARK

Ian Weber

ISBN
978-1-964035-85-7 (Paperback)
978-1-964035-84-0 (eBook)

Gifted PARK

TABLE OF CONTENTS

PART ONE

CHAPTER 1

Searching for Letitia among the bedraggled and exhausted souls proved more challenging than expected. The university gymnasium housed all manner of flotsam and jetsam of island society, a floating population of professors, students, sporting wannabes, or has-beens. These exercise junkies kept to a rigid policy of early morning or post-sunset workouts to manage the smothering humidity.

A few tentative steps forward and several expectant glances found her sitting atop a blue box at the far side of the room, surrounded by a gaggle of sweaty men. Her left leg was pulled up tightly against her body, and her arms were wrapped around it, with her chin resting comfortably on her knee. The right leg hung loosely over the edge of the box. It dangled a tantalising inch off the floor, slowly sweeping back and forth but never quite finding safety. The mesmerising, slow-moving pendulum seemed to match the rhythm of the music seeping from her phone.

My eyes followed the line of her body and exposed skin, with beads of sweat gliding slowly around the of her upper thigh and muscular calves. Bookending the curves were high-cut, all-black Converse sneakers and matching socks that almost blended seamlessly with her skin. My eyes tracked effortlessly from her elbow upward to her exposed shoulder. More beads of sweat caught in mid-stream as they made their way towards the trim of the black sports singlet.

The red headphone lead ran past her neck and down her stomach from the black Sennheiser headphones. Her leg hid the cord momentarily as it passed between her inner thighs, emerging briefly only to disappear again into the phone's jack hidden beside her foot. Her head rocked in time with the beat as her heel bounced lightly off the side of the box. The movements slowed a little as the playlist tracked to the next song.

She was singularly focused on the music and thoughts, oblivious to others around her. She lifted her head from her knee but continued to bob in time with the beat of the music. Not wanting to startle her, I approached from the front, stopping within arm's reach of her hunched body. But the music and the moment were hers. Nothing interrupted that focus. Not the movement or noise surrounding her.

Her head stopped bobbing abruptly. She picked up the phone and read a text. There was no way of making out what it said. She mumbled something, but it remained a part of the indistinctive chatter. Her shoulders, once relaxed, were now tensed, and her body rigid. It was as though the text had a life of its own, reaching out from the ether and strangling her peaceful moment into a lifeless existence. She took a breath and sighed as though exhaling deeply held frustration. I waited. Her attention focused on the phone as she launched into writing a text. Whatever she punched out was pure emotion, no thinking, an all-out attack. Whoever was reading this missile would feel that anger tracking across the keys.

For a moment, she paused, perhaps considering the consequences of the message. The thumb hovered above the 'send' key. Then, thinking turned to action. She cocked her head and twisted her neck, and an audible crunch let out the frustration. A short, sharp nod, and she punched the send key, bringing life to the response. Each gesture, coordinated and purposeful, added weight to the message as it tracked toward its target.

I cleared my throat, but Letitia did not respond. A hand on her knee brought her back from wherever she had gone. Her eyes flicked quickly from me to her phone, then back to me. She looked into my eyes but said nothing. Perhaps glancing at the phone was to make sure the message had been sent or a nervous response to the possibility the message had been seen. A gentle smile tried to reassure her, but again, there was no response. Perhaps no response is a response. It was.

There's certainty as to whether the incoming text or my tardiness set the tone. Perhaps it was too much to think 'island time' might work in one's favour. That would have been okay if she had followed such practices. But, like many things on the island, interpretation and actions do not always coexist simultaneously.

'What are you listening to?'

'You're late Jack!' she shouted above the pounding noise now coming from her earphones.

Okay, a poor choice. A look around the room tried to gauge the embarrassment the comment had drawn from those circling us. None could be measured, so on to grovelling and asking for forgiveness. It may not have been the best of the limited options available.

'Sorry, caught by the storm.'

A casual reference to the weather might have usually gotten some traction, but it quickly became apparent that excuses were off the table. Attempting to negotiate my way out of this predicament only brought a quicker and more decisive response.

'I booked the canvas for an hour, and we're already fifteen minutes late. You still have to get gloved up, headgear on, and warmed up. So, let's go!'

'We're doing boxing?'

'You wanted to work out, right,' she said. 'That's how I work out. You know I'm a much nicer person after boxing.'

'I'm more worried about during than after.' 'When you mentioned boxing, I thought you meant in a group or shadowboxing.'

Letitia rocked forward, grabbed the phone and my forearm, and pulled the headphones backwards with the other hand. The large foam earpieces and the band slipped over her platted hair, bobbled momentarily, and landed comfortably around her shoulders. From the earphones, Bob Marley's rhythmic tones cast out upon the air. The lyrics masked my concern. Perhaps every little was not alright, and I should be worried.

'I'm a big Marley fan,' I said, trying to work out a way to scavenge a little forgiveness. 'There's a huge poster of Marley on a dangerous curve in Koh Samui.'

'Yeah, yeah, great story,' she said. 'But we've got other things to do right now.'

Strike three. No forgiveness forthcoming. Note to self: don't be late again.

'Which ones?' Letitia said, thrusting two pairs of weathered boxing gloves into my stomach. 'Red or blue?'

It sounded like a simple enough question. Choose a colour. It should have been easy. It shouldn't matter, should it? How significant was the colour of the gloves? They were just gloves, right? Or was I missing something? I desperately wanted to relieve the tension before getting into the ring. After all, climbing onto the canvas with an angry person, even if it wasn't focused on me, was probably not wise. Give her a little time to work through whatever had pissed her off. But the flaccid contemplation at the significance of the colour of boxing gloves only managed to rile her even more.

She stuffed the red gloves into my hands. That indecision had set an uncertain future in motion. A flick of her head directed me to a tall, lean, Indian-looking man casually leaning against the ropes on the other side of the ring.

'You're wasting time,' she said. 'He'll get you ready.'

Short and not so sweet. Letitia turned and walked to the opposite corner, where another one of her friends waited. I looked at her trainer, smiled and nodded while Letitia grabbed a set of black gloves from her gym bag. The gloves glistened from the bright down lights above the ring. Without pausing, she slipped a glove over her right hand, tightening the Velcro fastener with her free hand. A quick flex of the gloved hand confirmed it was comfortable. Her friend helped with the other. Within moments, she was battle-ready. I stood with gloves in hand, far from ready and even more uncertain about what would come.

A hand rested on my shoulder. The trainer stood almost toe-to-toe. He took the gloves as smoothly as a pickpocket would have. His sharp, angular face and dark, brooding eyes stared back. Perhaps he was a man in his mid-twenties. It was a guess at best. There was no way of telling. Some cultures hide it well. His lean, wiry body complemented his almost robotic, purposeful movements. He flicked a look at me and then back to the equipment. There was something behind his eyes. It was difficult to determine what that was, but I admired it. He was powerful, confident, and reassured, looking like he could handle himself inside and outside the ring. Placing one of the gloves under his armpit, the trainer broke the Velcro seal on the other with his teeth and offered the glove. The trainer reached out and pushed the glove on a slightly trembling hand.

I became distracted again by movement in the ring. Letitia flexed both hands, but she wasn't happy with the tightness of the right glove. She called her friend over to adjust it and re-tighten the Velcro fastener. Another flex of both hands and the gloves crashed together to announce her readiness. My trainer was still negotiating the left glove, shoving the glove hard on my hand. I gestured to flex the gloves, as she had done, to get the fit just right.

'How does that feel? Tight?' the trainer asked, holding both gloved hands in front of me at waist height.

'Maybe a little too tight,' I responded.

'Good, that's how it should be,' the trainer said. 'Don't want your hands moving around inside. If they do, you'll surely break 'em. That's if you're lucky enough to hit her.'

There was no wink or gesture as if he was joking, which only increased my nervousness and growing concern. The trainer grabbed the black headgear from his khaki duffle bag at his feet and placed it on my head, pulling it down tight and slapping the top lightly to secure the fit. He pulled the Velcro strap under the chin tightly. He bent over again and searched inside his bag. He picked out a small white plastic case wrapped in plastic, a new mouthguard inside. He gestured for me to open my mouth, and I complied. He pushed the guard into my mouth, and I clamped down on it to ensure a comfortable fit, but it wasn't.

'Do I need all this?'

Most hobbled meanderings would be challenging to decipher, but the trainer had spent a lifetime around the ring. It was a language he knew all too well.

'Only if you want to keep your teeth in a row and your head on your shoulders,' the trainer said with a wry smile.

A simple yes would have sufficed. I'd become fond of both over the years and didn't want to lose either tonight. My thoughts tracked back over the last few minutes, and only one thing came to mind. What did the trainer mean by lucky enough to hit her?

Letitia was already in the ring, relaxed, standing with one arm over the top rope, the other gloved hand resting comfortably on her hip. Her right leg crossed over her left, steadfastly holding her body erect. A singular, unwavering demeanour flowed from her and across the ring. So confident. She was totally at home in this roped arena. A neck roll loosened the muscles, and then a series of purposeful stretches using the rope as leverage seemed part of a regular warm-up routine. She was ready, but was I? That wasn't even a consideration anymore.

The trainer placed one foot on the bottom rope and lifted the other to create a gap for me to step through without tripping. I felt the trainer's hand on my back, half guiding, half pushing me toward my destiny. After stepping into the ring, the ropes snapped back into place, sealing any possible retreat.

'Sparred much?' Letitia asked.

She was either gauging my level of boxing competency, or perhaps tensions had thawed. Maybe her relaxed and confident stance supported the latter, one hoped. After all, agreeing to a workout session was an excuse to spend more time with her. Such thinking had clouded any rational decision-making. Pride had gotten me this far; ego might just bury me. It seemed a simple enough question. Then why did I have to go and complicate the situation even more?

'Well, my sparring is usually limited to weekend retreats with wine and cheese.'

Such playfulness rolled effortlessly and irresponsibly from loose lips. As they floated across the canvas, a sudden realisation dawned. A chance to lighten the level of intensity might have achieved the opposite.

It seemed to be another miscalculation among a growing litany. Her eyes narrowed, shifting from non-committal to pro-homicidal. Pound-for-pound, she'd barely scratch the scales as a flyweight. But what she lacked in size and weight, she made up for in seemingly pissed-off rage. She swung around and walked to her corner, where her friend inserted a mouthguard. She looked over and rolled her shoulders forward, then backwards. But there was no advancing across the canvas. Instead, she stood rigid, like a soldier at attention. She raised her right glove slightly above her eye-line. With a chided grin opposing her mouthguard, she cocked the glove and flicked her hand forward twice, like knocking on a door.

'Ding, ding.' Letitia's muffled but comprehensible words floated across the canvas.

She leaned forward and pushed off with her back foot to gain momentum. As she did, her gloves collided, and a loud crack rang across the ring. With it, her tightly coiled body sprang into action, and whatever hell she would bring with the advance. I felt a chill run from my shoulders down a jaundiced spine. It was as though someone had walked upon my grave. That fate may not be too far in the future. It was becoming more apparent by the second that I'd made a severe miscalculation.

Letitia shifted to the left and began circling. The movement was both strategic and functional. It was clear who the hunter was and who the prey was. Shuffling back to the right, then to the left. I tried to counter each move, but she closed in a little each time her feet shuffled forward. It is best to be prepared. I moved the gloves up to cover my face. Protect the head and teeth from being knocked off and out at all costs.

There's a certain truth to boxing as an art and a science. So far, Letitia seemed to have advanced degrees in both. And she wasn't even wearing headgear. The trainer's comment may just be prophetic. Now more than halfway across the canvas and closing, she hesitated, pausing her advance momentarily as she dropped her guard. A reprieve. No! That was far too hopeful thinking. She started bouncing, shifting from one foot to the other. She was so light on her feet, dancing effortlessly to a mysterious beat. Her hair, heavy with the weight of her thick ponytail, flicked from side to side in sync with her steps, a mesmerising pendulum of dark curls.

Letitia was only a few feet away now but close enough for me to see a bead of sweat trickling down her forehead. It halted briefly above her left eyebrow, then curved effortlessly around the eye. What was hiding behind those beautiful dark brown eyes? Then, the realisation dawned. Any concern about the limited physical capacity to counter my opponent shifted to a lack of masculine control. I'd somehow become the living, breathing essence of the male gaze so eloquently assessed and dispatched in her thesis chapter. I couldn't remember how many times I'd run my mouth about gender equality in class, addressing students' indiscretions and guiding them towards a level of enlightened thinking. Blame could have been easily assigned to the testosterone-driven gym for such failings. But that didn't excuse those thoughts. It had become a simple and unequivocal reduction of her to a sexual object for pleasure and desire. Was it possible she was physically and intellectually superior to me? This consideration had the potential for resounding failure in this moment of truth and far beyond any relational objectives.

Shuffling from left to right opened a broader view of the ring and the onlookers who had tripled, as was the rising concern for my wellbeing. Backing out now was possible and probably wise. But then ego stepped in. And without thinking of the consequences, more drivel spewed from across the ring.

'Float like a butterfly and sting like a bee, perhaps, in your case, a fly,' I mumbled.

Surprisingly, there was little, if any, change in her demeanour. It was as though she hadn't heard or understood what was said. That was entirely possible, given the mouthguard-reduced clarity. The crowd went silent. Expectant. A now familiar dip of the head launched Letitia's tightly coiled body forward, and she floated across the canvas. Her feet barely touched the bouncy surface. A flurry of three or four air jabs erupted. That was, at best, an estimation. The flashes were so fast the count could have been more. It certainly wasn't less. Whatever the number, they were fast and coming quickly. The night would be over if just one of those lasered in on the chin.

If I hadn't blinked, I might have caught a better look at the right hook tracking toward my face. Not that it would have mattered much. I clumsily attempted to deflect the punch, but the effort was twenty years too late. A younger version probably wouldn't have even thought to get in the ring, let alone be here and in the line of fire. There was just enough time to close my eyes and brace for impact. It landed where it intended, crashing flush on the left side of my face, collecting my nose, cheek, and eye socket as it powered through its destructive arc.

At that moment, everything blackened, and consciousness and time slipped away. It could have been an hour, a minute, or a few seconds. In the haze of semi-consciousness, the audible gasps from onlookers were distinctive. It was a chorus of concern, horror, and admiration, all acknowledging the precision, power, and pinpoint accuracy.

A dark, indistinguishable shape hovered above. I blinked once, then again. Opening and closing the eyes was an attempt to clear the blurred vision. The dark form started to come into focus, but barely. She stood legs astride my limp body. There was little ability and even less willingness to respond. The left side of my face felt double the size as the pain ripped through my jaw and cheek. Lips, now inflated, issued a distinctive metallic taste. My tongue instinctively searched the inside of the cheek to locate the damage. It flicked at an overly large chunk of skin torn from the soft inner lining by teeth seeking shelter from the onslaught. Another gulp only revealed more blood. But that wasn't the only thing damaged.

Letitia leaned further over my prone body, lying at her feet. Her right arm curled; her muscular biceps wound tightly. I tried desperately to focus, and some sharpness of sight and mind had gradually returned. That must have been how Liston felt as Ali stood all-conquering over him, yelling, 'Stand up and fight!' But there was no fight to have then or now. Like Liston, it took only a moment to realise the devastation that punch had exacted. Gasps had been replaced by applause. Among the clearing haze, her lips moved, uttering a string of words as brutal as any of Ali's punches and taunts.

'Now, who's a funny man?' she zeroed in.

Even filtered through the mouthguard, the words complemented a conquering grin. Both could have easily been mistaken for smarmy or self-righteous, and for a good reason. Letitia had dismantled the weakest of defences and manhood in one precise blow. In that moment, there emerged a solemn truth of total domination.

Her tongue caressed her upper lip. It was as if she could taste my defeat. Sweet and delicious in flavour, satisfying in texture. But then came the subtlest of a wink, or was it a blink? Whatever it was, it was as fast as the punch she'd thrown. It could have easily been missed in the haze of recovering consciousness, shaded by a blinding headache that bleached deep in my muddled brain. She leaned over me even further; her face now seemed more relaxed. She had a sense of asserted calmness and control.

'You know I love ya, right?'

'Riiiiight,' was all I could slur from the uncertainty of unconsciousness.

Wait! What? I suddenly realised what she had said. She loved me. In one fluid motion, she stepped off to exit the ring. Though the number of spectators had dwindled, disappearing into the recesses of the gym, the adulation had not. A slow, careful, painful head roll helped to follow her exit. As she approached the ropes, her friend stepped on the lower one, and another person lifted the other, allowing her to step triumphantly through the gap. Slaps on the back welcomed her into the arms of supporters. But I maintained the vigil. All I needed was one look to confirm what I'd thought she said. A quick turn of the head, followed by a sweep of the ponytail, brushed away the possibility I'd misheard. A glance from the corner of her eye had somewhat erased the pain. It was short, sure, but it held my attention. Then she was gone, swallowed up by the crowd and the darkness of the gym. To my left, there was a bounce of footsteps on the canvas. The trainer leaned over, holding several fingers a few centimetres from a pulsating face.

'How many fingers?' The trainer yelled, and my eyes shifted from an out-of-focus face to his hands.

'You don't have to yell,' I responded. 'Four, no three. Give me a moment, and it might be two.'

'How many fingers?' the trainer repeated in a seemingly quieter, more concerned tone than the first time.

'Two, yes two, definitely two,' I lied.

'You mustn't be too rattled if you can joke about it,' the trainer said. 'You're okay, I think.'

Saying someone is okay is a relative term, especially if you're the one lying prone on the canvas. The number of fingers didn't matter in the scheme of things. He was wrong, though, I decided. The comment was less about humour and more about embarrassment. It is strange how those two can seem the same. The trainer offered an outstretched hand, a gesture gently declined. More time was needed before going vertical. A glance at the trainer was met with a broad smile ripped knowingly across his face.

'Ain't love grand?'

'Sorry, what?

'Imagine if she didn't love you,' the trainer said. 'Boy, you would have taken a hell of a beating.'

There was no smart quip, no cute comeback. I slowly rolled my head from side to side and gently massaged my jaw with a still-gloved hand. I desperately wanted the persistent ringing to stop. Such sounds weren't new. Bouts of vertigo and the inevitable tinnitus made for an uncomfortable familiarity. But this was different. It wasn't an intermittent buzzing. Instead, it was more like a high-pitched scream seeping through each synapse. It took a minute, maybe two, but the ringing gradually dissipated. Perhaps one positive had come from this disaster. Maybe accepting the luck of a quick defeat echoed the preciousness of life itself. Rolling to one side onto the elbow allowed the trainer to grab my arm and waist to help him to my feet. But going vertical only accentuated the pain in a battered face.

'Do you have anyone who can check on you?' the trainer asked. 'Just in case you have a concussion.'

'It's fine,' I lied again through aching jaw and teeth.

CHAPTER 2

A shower and change of clothes would have made the aching face moderately bearable. Finding a box close to the changing room to rest was easy, but getting comfortable was more difficult. It had only been ten minutes, but the once-crowded foyer had dwindled to a handful of exhausted faces. Semi and Ruben busily organised the closing of the gym.

'Hey Jack, I got your membership card,' Semi said.

It wasn't important but it was a distraction, welcome or not. I took the card and walked a few steps.

'My last name is spelt G-R-A-H-A-M and there should be a Dr in the front.'

Semi gave Ruben a glancing look of disapproval. He didn't have say a word to his little brother at that moment but that might come later.

'I'll make sure it's right next time you're in.'

A tentative caress of the lip with the thumb confirmed the damage, and it was impossible to avoid repeatedly finding the gashed inner cheek and tongue. The bleeding had stopped, but the metallic taste remained as much as the lingering bitterness of defeat.

As minutes ticked by, thoughts shifted to explaining the battered, swollen face to students. They'd notice, of course, and it would be the talk of the class if not the university already. Ripped straight from the headlines: *PROFESSOR TASTES BITTER DEFEAT.* By tomorrow, it would be much worse. It felt like the eye was about to explode from its socket. Maybe just tell the truth. But there would be no redemption in that. What was needed was a way to save face. Ironical, as it was. After all, the best truths I've ever heard were someone else's lies. It was the right time for some home-spun disinformation, but my brain wasn't cooperating, nor were the people exiting the changing rooms.

Each creak of the shower room door was a welcomed distraction and immediate disappointment. What was taking her so long? Ten more minutes passed, then twenty. There is no way it should take this long. A familiar voice boomed from behind the reception desk.

'Closing up shop in five,' Semi said.

The voice, deep and guttural, echoed throughout the empty crevices of the gymnasium: no music, no clanging of weights, or the whirring of treadmills to lighten its tenor. And still, no Letitia.

'Just waiting for my conqueror to finish up,' I said, hoping he'd not take a cheap shot.

I needn't have worried.

'Oh, she left immediately after,' Ruben responded from the other end of the front desk.

'You sure?'

'Yeah, I took her locker key, and she left,' he said. 'Didn't shower, just left.'

That made no sense. Why would she take off like that? No wallowing in victory, not even a goodbye. I quickly searched my bag at the foot of the box and found my phone. Pressing the home button brought it to life. But it was a barren landscape flickering incomprehensively before me. No messages. Just two missed calls, neither from her. The voicemails offered a couple of apologies, such as 'I can't make class tomorrow' messages and the familiar excuses from the usual suspects. One day, maybe, those excuses might become a little more creative.

A churning feeling started to well up. Uncertainty and nervousness weighed heavy. Those thoughts rolled out a bunch of possible scenarios for why she'd left in a rush. Perhaps it was an emergency, or she was late for something else. My delay didn't help. No wonder she was annoyed.

But the whole thing lasted less than twenty minutes, mostly getting in and out of the ring and now waiting another half hour for her, and she wasn't even here.

Those moments ushered in far less pleasant thoughts. Had I blown any chance with her? Was this all just a game? Why did she leave? Uncertainty turned to neurotics.

The gymnasium's curved furrows and ridges of grey corrugated metal skin that wrapped effortlessly around the low-set structure seeped quickly into the darkness of the campus. A freshness in the night air cooled by the ocean breeze didn't lift my spirits. A uniformed guard opened his eyes and leaned out through the open section of the campus security hut. A glance and a nod were enough. Dodging the roadworks created a more stable path to home.

The light breeze bit deeper into my sweat-laden chest. That chilled feeling would usually bring some relief, but not tonight. Inner turmoil wrestled its way to less pleasant thoughts. It became less of a walk and more of a trudge to the apartment as anger replaced concern. As those feelings seeped deeper, so too did the shame. My ego had taken a beating, more than anyone would care to admit, but anger. Why anger? THAT'S PURE BULLSHIT! A scream reverberated within my turmoil, heard by no one but entirely deafening.

That was the same stupidity she'd fought so hard to drag herself away for so long. That's not the promise we made to each other. Pushing those thoughts aside took some heavy lifting. But they were soon replaced by others.

Was this my moment of truth, a test of character? With more thinking came more uncertainty. Was this all part of the greater evolutionary plan? Was this the way to be selected from the gene pool simply by not matching her physical prowess in the ring?

Calling it a pool was perhaps a little generous. At forty years old, it was more of a shallow puddle. Indeed, her emphatic knockout could be an exclamation point to that evolutionary decline. I'd imagined this moment so differently, far more poetically or creatively. It played out as two courting eagles soaring high on the updrafts to high altitude, swooping toward each other, crashing together at high speed. Talons entwined, whirling through the air as they spiral toward the ground, disengaging moments before impact. But that thinking had been quickly replaced with the harsh reality. There was the impact, sure enough – her glove, my face, and me lying prone and semi-conscious on the canvas. It wasn't poetic at all. And it certainly wasn't romantic. What it was, well, fucking brutal. Instead of soaring eagles, it was like two mating hyenas, with the dominant female choosing her mate, copulating furiously, holding the life force within, and discarding her partner ruthlessly. Unwanted, useless. Seed sown; deed done. It seemed like Darwinism at its selective best, or worst in this case.

As that realisation hit home, each step seemed like quicksand. Only the faint glimmer of apartment lights held the hope of a reprieve from the weight of self-loathing. The apartment oozed comfort and peace, an oasis from the heat and a secure place to call home. Something I'd yearned for all my life. It allowed for a quiet existence with friendly neighbours, rarely seen. And the landlord, a sweet old man, told the best stories of adventures as a young man when we crossed paths. Some might have tired of the old man's stories, but I sought them out and encouraged him at every opportunity. Sometimes, the old man would tell the same story, each with a bit of change to the details. The nuanced, changing facts did not affect the outcome but enhanced the journey.

One of my favourites was when he'd shaken Charles Kingsford-Smith's hand when he landed on the island for a fuel stop during a trans-Pacific crossing. He was just three years old, but seeing an aircraft for the first time matched the importance of meeting this adventurer, which had not been lost over time. The old man reminded me of my long-lost grandfather. There was no comparison in looks but certainly in character and the grace with which he approached life.

I remember my Pops so vividly on the old farm. He would walk silently to the edge of the stables, sit down, hunched over, and start rolling a cigarette. I would follow along with the two blue heelers. I'd watch his calloused, yellowed fingers pluck tobacco from a small steel box and grind the loose leaves with the palm of his hand. He would stretch out the rolled tobacco, place it in a white, loose-leaf Tallyho paper, and then roll it into a cigarette with one hand. It was magical to watch the dexterity of a seventy-year-old man, but having smoked since he was fourteen, Pops was long past 10,000 repetitive movements for mastery of the long-lost skill. A light lick along the length of the paper sealed its contents. He'd tongue one end and spit out the outlying remnants of an over-filled cigarette while striking a match. The flame curled around the end of the cigarette, and a heavy draw filled his lungs.

A rush of exhaled, blue smoke carried the story's first word as though one couldn't survive without the other. Each story made the stooped old man seem larger than life, almost unbelievable, as his stories rolled effortlessly along the train of smoke. It mattered not if the stories were true. The imagery and fine detail were reminiscent of a custodial watercolour – a picture painted with vivid artistry, a creation far from the mundane. Like the old man's stories, the experience was profound. I'd never wanted to live an ordinary life but an extraordinary one. It had become not a matter of choice but of purpose and destiny.

Storytelling became the stock and trade. One world adventure after another built the foundations of artistic endeavour and so much more. I am sure my grandfather would be proud of how the young storyteller had created worlds of astonishing detail that touched the lives of others. Such stories could and should change humanity for the better. Each one is an endeavour of worthiness. Like those childhood stories, they didn't have to be true. They only needed a kernel of truth to be spun into a mythic tale to capture the reader.

But such creations relied on memory and brain power, now in limited supply, consumed by my struggle to ease the lingering pain in my brain. A search for both only tracked back to the pain each step exposed mercilessly. What was needed, perhaps, was empathy. Conjuring that from a bunch of twenty-year-olds was a tough ask at the best of times. Getting them to talk coherently about their feelings was challenging unless they related to some existential crisis they were experiencing in the here and now. Perhaps sympathy might play right and true if done well. But both were undeserved. So complete was the loss, the beat down. There was little to salvage for a believable story that explained the battered and bruised face. The spark of creativity that had momentarily flickered had now extinguished.

Ideas of saving face shifted to changing pace. A left into the back laneway to the apartment was met with the sound of the ocean lapping against the cement wall at the edge of Apted Park. Just a few more steps in the darkened laneway gave way to an opening in the thick, overgrown hedge surrounding the back side of the property. A flash of headlights from behind sliced through gaps in the hedge, lighting the darkened tree-lined interior of the apartment complex. The beams cast garish shadows against the building's back wall and stairs. Navigating these would be a little easier tonight. The challenge would be climbing to the top before the headlights passed. But they didn't pass. Two steps at a time and fumbling for the keys occupied the short time to scale the stairs. Standing square with the iron security gates, I heard footsteps on the path below. That was strange. The neighbours should be asleep by now or at least inside watching television.

Ignoring the approaching footsteps, I unlocked the first steel security gate with two clicks as the deadbolt released. The creak of steel-on-steel sounded the gate's reluctance to comply. I placed the key back in the lock and, with a quick turn, secured the gate. A shadow near the stairs caught my attention. Maybe it was Letitia. Peering through the bars revealed no one. But I sensed a presence. Over the years, one important lesson was learned. Nothing good ever came from an unexpected person arriving at an unexpected time, incredibly late at night. Shifting my weight to the left leg, I careened further than I thought possible. There was only darkness, no movement now, no shadows, no noise other than the trees rustling from the light ocean breeze. A second key unlocked the remaining security gate. This opening one was a little trickier. It took some time to work out how to release the catch, but a slight jiggle to the left released the misaligned mechanism. It clicked on command, and a grating sound let out as the door swung open.

One of the benefits of steel-grilled windows was that they could be left ajar during the day and night, allowing the apartment to cool quickly without fear of someone breaking in. Of course, there were good reasons why apartments, particularly in this area, were secured in such a secure way. Such measures harkened back to when lawlessness raged rampantly after the island coups, making for a fearful community. Police struggled to maintain law and order. Gangs of youths roamed the streets of outlying suburbs, beating and robbing anyone they encountered. Newspapers and television news reported rapes and murders. So, steel grills became a necessity.

It only took a few steps inside the apartment to feel the cool inner sanctum engulf my battered soul. There was a slight pause at the doorway to place the umbrella against the wall and turn the fan to full speed. The blades launched into action with a deep groan, redistributing the air quickly throughout the apartment. Outside was thirty-plus degrees and one hundred plus per cent humidity, but the barometer near the door read twenty-eight degrees. There was no significant difference, but every degree counted in the scheme of comfort control.

The sweaty clothes fell quickly to the floor on the way to the bathroom. A refreshing shower was just a few steps away. Hopefully, that might wash away what had been less than a spectacular end to the day. I adjusted the temperature and flow of water as it spurted from the shower rose. Bliss.

Through the small window in the cubicle, I could hear the car accelerate from the back entrance along the laneway towards the settlements that split the island's haves and have-nots. A flick of the gears from second to third sent the car speeding along Fletcher Road toward Vatuwaqa.

PART TWO

CHAPTER 3

I moved from my transit hotel in late summer to the second-floor apartment of a blue and white, two-level building that backed onto Hutson Laneway. Each morning, the weak light of the civil dawn filters through the large, white-slatted louvres fronting Beach Road and Apted Park, a small cuneate of land buffering the great blue expanse stretching out from Suva to the eastern horizon. These first rays cast a beguiling, warm touch upon the apartment. But it was not a place to linger. The super-charged rays make umbrellas bloom, and blooms wither as the sun moves past six degrees and breaches the horizon. It was as if God's first withering breath had been cast upon the slumbering earth.

I leaned over the wrought iron balcony and watched the remnants of the passing storm roll slowly out to the horizon. The clear, calm water of the Pacific laps against the edge of the knee-high stone wall, which fortified the park and the comfortable small, low-slung bungalows and colonial homes from tidal surges. The park is a lifeless track of lush green land during weekdays. On weekends, it becomes an oasis of activity as families enjoy sedate picnics and other romantic dates. From mid-Saturday morning, cars crawled along Beach Road, seeking any available parcel of parking real estate. Unbeknownst to these visitors, the nights in the park can be more interesting, depending on your palette. Shrilled voices call out from beyond the tall, curved palm trees, each pushed westward towards the city by relentless trade winds.

Drops of rain fell from the palm leaves to the grassed areas lining the edge of the park and footpath into glassy pools of water that had formed randomly on the road. I looked across the bay to the flow of inessential houses, water, and rocky outcrops that once flowered for British sailors' eyes—a fresh, fertile breast of the new world. Today, the bay harbours a raft of Chinese fishing and cargo boats seeking refuge from months at sea. Downtown bars would be busy tonight, filled with sailors seeking comfort in other ways.

A sudden flash in the distance drew my attention back to the passing storm. A three-second count between flash and thunder echoed from a distance, and then silence. It was gone as quickly as the storm rolled over the island and unleashed giant waterfalls onto the corrugated rooftop. Most called the torrential downpours *big rain*, but it would have been more accurate to call it *fat rain*, heavy with the weight of surprise for those hapless victims caught under its shade.

I took a deep breath and took in the fragrance of warm earthiness. Each droplet breaks down the geosmin molecules, releasing its aromatic compounds into the air. Its fragrance seemed all too familiar but still challenging to describe. I tried to guess its aroma; it had a clean, crisp intoxication. It was not quite herb-like, it was more like a spice. Maybe cinnamon or something else. It conjured childhood memories of afternoon thunderstorms and heavy rain on the dusty cane fields, barking dogs, and tractors roaring to life somewhere in the distance. Home lingers large no matter how far you run.

A vibration drew my hand to my jean pocket. The message was short, 'Where are you?' None of those unnecessary pleasantries you find these days. The rain was no longer a consideration as urgency filled my thoughts. I didn't respond. I slotted the phone into my rain jacket pocket and the keys from the hook beside the fan controller. I locked the security gates, steading my descent to negotiate the slippery stairs.

'Hey, Jack,' came a voice behind the heavily meshed door. 'Got a minute?'

'Not really, Phil, running late.'

'You got a class? It'll only take a second.'

It was as though the shortness of time somehow negated the level of urgency. Not surprisingly, it never takes a second, ever. From behind the screeching screen door emerged a familiar balding head, a jaundiced arch hallowed with warm tones of the corridor light cascading from above. It wasn't a flattering look, lit or not. This apartment was the only one of four screened for mosquitos. Only a chance meeting on campus revealed why such steely defences were necessary, not a privilege. What transpired that day could have been described as a movable feast with Phil squarely on the menu. A swarm of mosquitos set about devouring their prey, each one gathered at the table hungry and ready. Among the visual pleasantries was an unchoreographed mix of Gaelic dancing and self-flagellation as Phil took umbrage at being the main course. It amused those passing by who hadn't realised the irony at play. His wife was the UN mosquito doctor appointed to the eradicate the very nemesis that sought his demise.

'Tell me you heard the commotion last night in the park?' Phil said. 'It woke me, so you must have heard it up top. Some guy went all George Michael in the toilets and got arrested.'

It would have been rude to fob him off. He'd become a friend of sorts, or at least a friendly distraction. You couldn't help feeling sorry for the guy and his hermit-like existence; too afraid to venture out, too settled to try. Along the way, books, booze and banter had been exchanged. But his self-imposed sentence had also nurtured a dark attraction to '90s cop shows and idle gossip. Self-preservation is one thing, hypocrisy is another. For me, history was firmly on the side of the non-gossipers.

'No,' I lied.

A lie only works as a cooperative act of deception. It has no substance whatsoever in its utterance, and it takes someone else to agree with the lie to give it power. It might have been the shifting of weight, a suspicious head tilt, or a direct stare that screamed eternal 'Liar!'

'Are you saying my ears lied? Phil said, 'I know what I heard. I just didn't see what you saw.'

'You're such a gossip,' I replied.

'Passes the time,' Phil responded. 'That's not an answer. Come on, what did you see from up there?'

'Ok, it woke me, or I was awake. I'm unsure which one, but I saw what was happening.'

'And?'

'As you said, the police pinned a handcuffed bald guy to the car's bonnet. It wasn't you, was it? No, it couldn't have been you. Wrong shine.'

'Funny,' Phil said. 'Did you see his face? Foreigner or local? Come on, just a little information. I'm so bored. Wait, what do you mean wrong shine?'

'I'm pretty sure boredom is not a requisite for gossiping.'

'You aren't as bored as I am,' Phil responded. 'It might be the only reason people gossip. Did you think of that? Wait, you know who it is, don't you? He's from the university, or well-known at least, right?'

'Why do you say that?'

'You're as boring as I am. You go to the university and come home, and that's your life. You never go out other than to shop, and hardly anyone visits. So, I think he's a university person. Come on, who is it?'

'That's a little creepy. When you're walking on a beach with a beautiful woman, and you're the only person who thinks you're together, it's called stalking.'

'Don't deflect,' Phil pleaded. 'Give me something. Don't make me beg.'

'Begging's ok,' I said. 'But that would be as horrible as it would be uncomfortable. Tell me, how does this gossip thing work? Do you hang out on Thursdays at the Y? Is there a prize for the juiciest snippet?'

'Something like that.'

'You do? That was a pretty good guess.'

'Actually, you're closer than you think,' Phil responded.

'Oh, I can imagine a lot, and some,' I said. 'Comes with the territory.'

'Let's say it's a party of interested and similarly bored people gathering for mutual fulfilment from other people's mistakes and faux pas.'

'Gossips! You know there's a German word for that, *schadenfreude*; the pleasure one derives from another's misfortune.'

'*Ich weiß was es bedeutet,*' Phil replied without a hint of self-indulgence. 'And I know stuff about you too that's pretty juicy.'

'Oh, you do,' I said, surprised more with the German than the possibility my life was that interesting to anyone else. 'We need to get into that one day. So, where does this like-minded gaggle meet? Down at the local supermarket, or OneRepublic for a coffee and a slice of gossip?'

'Actually, pretty much exactly that.'

'Look, I don't think it's up to me to say. I'm sure you'll hear about it in the local rag, or maybe not,' I said.

'I don't think you get the point of gossiping in knowing about something before everyone else does,' Phil said. 'But my spider senses picked up on that little hint there. I think he's a local and someone well-known, too. Oh, this is going to be good. I can feel a tingle in my nether regions.'

'Disgusting as that is intriguing,' I said. 'Are you sure it's not malaria?'

'Don't do that.'

'What?'

'A guy gets arrested not 40 metres from my apartment for indecent exposure in the local convenience, and I'm expected to let it ride? Not going to happen.'

'Do you think it's possible to have decent exposure in a public place and not get arrested?' I poked back.

'No, come on. You know who the perp is.'

'Perp!' I responded. 'You gotta stop watching so many of those American cop shows. Which season of CSI, SVU are you binge-watching? You need to lather up and get out more.'

'Law and Order SVU. It's 22 seasons, and don't piss all over the New York Police Department. They are the last line of defence between the animals and us. Besides, you know what I'm watching. You gave me the goddamned boxed set, and you won't tell me, will you?'

'Give me a good reason why I should. Put your investigator hat on that too-inquisitive brain of yours and get deducing. It's worth the effort. Trust me.'

'Oh, nice, building the intrigue. Represent. Good work. But I don't need more motivation. And look at you, pushing the gossip button.'

'Nice chat,' I said as I stepped off the bottom stair to the cement footpath that tracked out to the back laneway. 'Let's talk again soon. Update me on your investigation post-get-together.'

The voice and the footsteps trailed into the darkness, followed by inaudible grumblings and the screen door slamming shut and the corridor light extinguished. It would have been much easier to tell him who it was, but more fun to Hansel and Gretel a trail he could follow. Besides, if it weren't Phil, it'd be someone else. Secrets don't stay secrets long on this island. Everybody knows what everybody is doing, even if they are doing it with the right people.

I breached the inner sanctum of the apartment compound but stopped suddenly. The larger pools of water could be avoided quite easily, but the smaller ones were the most treacherous for twisted ankles or worse. Launching from one dry spot to another was not the most elegant of dances, and it would have been a strange sight for anyone watching from the houses fronting the other side of the laneway. Each leap and bound down along the laneway had none of the grace of a ballerina. Reaching safer ground was at the expense of dry clothes saturated in sweat.

Passing the bus stop revealed no people and no bus. It was not a good sign for speeding up the journey to campus. Catching a bus was more good luck than prudent planning. If you turned up and a bus was nearby, you were in luck, with the schedule running on island time. Waiting for one wasn't an option. Drowning in your sweat was suffocating, so making it to the next stop was the goal. You didn't have to watch for one sneaking up from the rear. The green glassless monsters announced their arrival far off into the distance before they could be seen. Reggae music pounding out at total volume from the windowless carriages. It remained a mystery that this music had such a hold so far from its roots. Someone once casually mentioned it inspired the local struggle against the colonial oppressors. That may be true, but that battle had been won fifty years earlier. No matter the outcome, it spoke to them, and they listened to it in deafening tones. Maybe it was played loudly to hide the creaks and moans of the old British Leyland-made warhorses. Whatever the reason, there was no music and no bus.

Construction of the new walkway near campus had taken far longer than it should have, as things often do here. It barely stretched out a hundred metres from the university entrance, though what was there was welcomed. It required a slight deviation from the road to the footpath. But the closeness of the destination was not the completeness of the journey. Negotiating campus security would see another delay, depending on who was on duty. One security guard loved a chat. Maybe it was just his way. Out of these interactions, a friendship of sorts had grown. Each time, we exchanged a little more of our personal lives. But today was not the day for extended banter.

The security hut split the entry-exit lanes of the campus. Placing security at only the main entrance seemed more ceremonial than functional. Checking identities was never a priority, with most people simply passing through with a nod or half-hearted wave. Such flaccid attempts to keep the learners in and the riffraff out didn't always work. It wasn't easy to tell the difference at times. That didn't mean passing through the 'checkpoint' would go unnoticed today. Someone was always inside—not necessarily awake or attentive–but there.

Not enough could be seen inside the hut to know who was on duty, and there might be a chance to slip by without being noticed. From the darkness of the hutch came an orb-shaped face with a smile like a waxing crescent moon blossoming against the dark sky. Like most past their early thirties, the man was overweight, if not obese. Indulging in traditional potatoes, taro and cassava meals had bolstered his girth and health issues. Each one is consumed far too often and in far too much quantity. With a familiar, laconic nod and wave of the hand, he took the lead in an all too familiar dance.

'Morning, Prof.'

'Morning, Bob.'

Bob wasn't his name. Remembering faces wasn't a problem. Names, on the other hand, posed a considerable challenge. There was no way that 'mate' or 'buddy' felt right. So, he became Bob. It didn't bother him, or maybe it did, but he was too polite to ask for a correction.

Most times, acknowledging him was enough, as few seemed to do. Foreigners did themselves no favours by not engaging with the locals. It seemed like it didn't matter, but it did. Yeah, the relationship was built around deception, but the forging of a bond of sorts appeared, in part, a good way to contradict the pedestrian nature of such relationships. The notion of hierarchy was important, so breaking such protocol seemed to ease the path to friendship. Honestly, anything was better than 'boss', as many had adopted when interacting with foreigners. It was just far too colonial and superior, and made me uncomfortable. Unfortunately, it was far too familiar in former British colonies. All had been scarred permanently by those who'd ruled the lands, powers that had ushered in regimented subservience and obedience to the King or Queen, and England. Most had suffered at the expense of their culture, resources, and dignity. Others hadn't resisted, carving out a productive trade and commerce relationship with those in power. They'd learned from history.

The inevitable departure of the colonials changed the leaders, not the power structure: new rulers, laws, obedience. The dictators struggled to lay claim to the throne. Their tenure lasted only if the military's patience held firm. Round after round of political upheaval— so regular, disruptive, and destructive. It scarred the people and the islands' reputation. Such disruptions descended into new levels of absurdity as one group toppled the other. Each one fell unceremoniously to the claims of Indigenous injustices. It had reached a point that the international community referred to it as 'coup-coup-land'. But such absurdity never dulled the smiles of its people, nor their banter.

'How's the wife, Prof?'

'Still divorced!'

'Sorry to hear that.'

'Still married?' I responded in kind.

'Yeah.'

'Sorry to hear that.'

'Me too,' he whispered, as though his wife might hear.

The response was a desperate mix of despair and resolution that nothing had or would ever change. He had accepted his marital fate. Much like his ancestral cousins, he was living a life of bonded indenture–yes, of his choosing. But one could offer some sympathy for his daily struggle against the torment of a never-ending existential crisis. I could relate to his plight somewhat, but I wasn't sure sympathy should be directed at Bob or his wife. Maybe it was simply a reflection of his failed marital experience. It was impossible to imagine or understand his specific situation, nor was there much interest in doing so. Such interactions had been short, and today would be no different. Other urgent things pressed for attention.

Time is far from a priority for islanders until it is. Ironically, it takes time to feel comfortable with their responses to it as a relative concept, not a defining practice. For those, life's existence revolved heavily around temporality, not formality. And when time-shifted unexpectedly, even minutely, sensibilities cascaded out of control. That transition hadn't frustrated me as much as it did others. I ensured the three Cs to survival were quickly in place–connect, communicate, and comfort. But I hoped island time would be his friend today; such was the daily commute to campus.

Each university is different. Some are old, steeped in tradition, ageing buildings, and even more senior professors. Others searched for an identity, a distinct look and energy. This one was neither and both. Its lush, flourishing palm leaves hung heavy from the constant rain. Here, you lived the age-old saying of watching grass grow, and it seemed like it needed cutting hourly. Filling gaps between buildings, open-air eateries, and old architecturally challenged cement-boxed buildings splashed with pastel colour. The only saving grace was a funky new performance centre and student and staff bungalows dotted across campus to no apparent design. But one building between the library and the health centre stood out, not just because of its large *Bure* design, but because it housed the only good coffee shop on campus.

It was perfectly placed just a minute from my office. Picking up student assignments would have been the prudent thing to do, but they weren't going anywhere. Some addictions must be appeased, otherwise, the chaotic world of learning would unravel. I was sure of that. It wasn't worth the risk, and I continued to the coffee shop. Besides, it would ease the pain of the inevitable student queries, staffing and resource issues and daily backstabbing, even temporarily. I was in luck as the line for service was short. Iced macchiatos and tropical fruit drinks took far longer to prepare. Patience. Worth it!

'Hey, Prof,' came the welcoming voice and smile from behind the café counter. 'Usual?'

I peered above the white Italian-made coffee machine and stainless steel-rimmed brackets holding the rows of freshly washed cups sitting securely on its stainless-steel top. I came for the coffee but stayed for the smile.

'Perfect,' I responded, handing across a five-dollar note. 'Nina, you're a lifesaver, a queen of addictions.'

She went to hand me the change, but I waved it away and pointed to the tips jar at the end of the serving area. It looked a little lean. Even a bit of change meant more to a struggling student. Besides, my pockets were laden with useless shrapnel. I retreated through the large, open doors. It looked like no one had used the plastic seats lined up under the sliver-thin wooden ledge that stretched out the length of the veranda. It could only accommodate a cup and saucer or maybe a book.

Two men stood at the corner of the leaf-shaped extension that tapered to a sharp point. I ignored them, though I recognised the shorter one. A quick brush of the ledge surface released the dust and leaves. Outside, there was no breeze, not even from the mosquito's wings constantly buzzing at my ear. A casual wave brushed aside the sound, knowing the gesture would only send the annoyance in search of another warm-blooded landing. The view of branches and leaves of the low-slung trees and the lush green gully helped ease my wait. The barely audible murmurs occasionally broke the sereneness of silence from the end of the veranda and from inside. Then, a voice leaked from the side where the men had been standing.

'Professor Graham!'

I desperately wanted to ignore the approach, but that wouldn't be possible. It never was with Ashet. There was no filter between silent and audible thoughts with him, as though everyone needed to know what was going on in that bald orb. But not everyone wanted to listen or engage. It seemed like I was the object of pursuit. That feeling of being the quarry made me uneasy. So, I simply imagined Ashet as the most minor and least threatening thing. For me, his look wouldn't been out of place lurking at the bottom of a garden, an overseer of little importance. For others, he was modern-day Napoleon in unfulfilled size and aspiration. But such ambitions involved slightly less in land grab and far less in leadership ability. But he did have one gift – don't we all – an opportunist with a talent for identifying who could advance his career. Ashet latches on to anyone with power, like a Remora, for protection and sustenance. So, it was wise to take care when he was around. Otherwise, you might end up becoming the meal. But I'd done my homework. What I'd discovered made perfect sense. Ashet had an older brother who had frequently received their mother's attention, which made the young boy obsessively assertive and driven by a desperate desire for approval. He was bullied at school, and an incident in the local convenience store scarred him for life. The trauma he'd tried to hide from most had not escaped all.

'I've been reading about Jacques Derrida,' Ashet continued, expecting no reply. 'You must know his work?'

'I've read his work,' I responded, manoeuvring to counter Ashet's position of superiority.

'Fascinating stuff, and I think you'd greatly benefit from his ideas. Expand your thinking.'

It was as if he hadn't heard my response over his inflated thoughts. Then there was that grating tone. The initial feeling was to reach out and extinguish the buzz of his voice. But Nina arrived in time to interrupt my murderous intent. She apologised for interrupting, but I waved that politeness away. She had not only handed me my coffee but an excuse to leave, and I took it.

'Class awaits,' I said, standing to limit Ashet's position on the high ground. 'You know how it is.'

He didn't. Ashet's issues were far more profound than his lack of physical stature and questionable intellect. He'd tried twice to earn a doctorate, one from Australia and the second at home. Both times, he flamed out in the proposal stage, blaming others for his failure. But it was more than that. There had to be something else that irked him more than just a bad review of his work. But I had no interest in finding out. Not now or in the future.

A quick check of the coffee lid secured the contents for the short trip. I set out through the café, calculating the fastest escape through the haphazardly placed tables and chairs. The layout changed daily, with students shifting furniture to accommodate group size–one table with eight chairs, another with none. An escape route came into view. It would take a little navigating, but the plan had its faults. Halfway to the exit, several familiar faces lingered in the jumbled seating. Six students – four from the writing class–sat crowded at a table, computers out. Hopefully, they were working on assignment drafts, but the reality was probably Facebooking – if that could be considered grammatical evolution.

Were they there before? Easy to miss. Say hello, I thought. It's polite, if not a necessity. It often seemed more like a game with students who demanded attention. The university appeased that call with teachers forced to be both support staff and educators. Maybe they were the same thing. Times had changed. They needed to be prepared for the real world. Harsh and relenting as it was. Instead, they were wrapped in cotton wool with stroked egos, releasing them into a world unprepared for what lay ahead. They looked up and smiled friendly-like. They held such innocence in their faces and were far too shy to say anything. No more time-wasting. Perfect!

I noticed the eyes of the four tracked to the collection of papers tucked under my arm, expectantly hoping for those to be marked assignments. They'd be disappointed to know they weren't. Nothing for you today, or soon, for that matter. So intense was the look, desperate to ask the question. But they knew better than to dip their toes into that murky well so early in the morning. The rule had been set—coffee first, chatter later.

Attention shifted to exiting around the remaining tables and chairs. Instead of the sanctuary of the office, the destination deviated to the administration office. It was early enough to grab the assignments without stumbling across errant staff. The expectant fragrance from the cup was the only company worth keeping as I made my way along the path. Its ubiquitous aromatic particles infused anticipation for the rest of the day. But it only piqued my interest right now. There'd be no pleasure in sipping its contents just yet. The bitterness would fortify the day as it had so many times before. Reliable and reassuring to be true.

CHAPTER 4

It was tempting to delay the retrieval of assignments and opt for a quieter, less stressful start to the day. Perhaps a sliver of guilt motivated me to retrieve their submissions instead of delaying it. I'd always thought of guilt as such a worthless feeling. I never enough to change a person's direction; only enough to bring you to cross-roads, unable or unwilling to take one path or the other.

Today, they'd need to decide on their destination–imagine their future and write their obituary. Capture their future selves and describe it as lived experience. That'd test anyone's creative talent and a more significant challenge for twenty-somethings with minimal life experiences. Well, none that'd help them with this task. What they didn't, or couldn't yet realise, was that life itself would hijack their hopes and dreams, sending them spiralling in unexpected directions. That'd be a life lesson each would have to learn on their terms. For now, they could wade into the uncomfortable knee-deep waters of anticipation. Sink or swim; the writing pool lay two flights up.

The bland, L-shaped building at the edge of campus wasn't new, so it possessed none of the comforts of thoughtful design. It housed two schools, education and law, arts and media, a loose cannon of disciplinary predilections. Whomever thought that law, arts and media belonged together should have asked someone before they made that decision. Picasso once said you must destroy before you can create.

That's fine for revolutionising art, literature, and architecture. But with revolution comes winners and losers. Melding disparate literary-type groups managed only to magnify the disciplinary differences and resulting disputes. Despite the infighting, backstabbing and personal political power plays, the creative sections of the school flourished, mainly due to the astute hires by the Head of the School. But along with accolades came accountability.

The first floor housed the law faculty among the recently renovated offices. A place of prestige they desperately craved. Entry to the reception area would not have been out of place in any law firm. Behind that façade, the Dean held centre stage among the plush surroundings. Polished oak bookshelves lined the edges of the office, each leather-bound law volume unread and untested, it seemed. Each component was designed to impress more than enlighten.

The education faculty had seconded themselves in the penthouse on the third floor. It was rare air, mainly because it was rare for anyone to be there. Most had some connection to the Dean—blood or favour. Sandwiched between these two were the literati, writers and filmmakers, a collection of creatives more interested in disobedience and revolution led by a self-proclaimed poet, Laurette, and a political animal. Access to the administration office lies in the middle offices on the second floor.

Two flights of stairs could be easily managed at a brisk pace. Polite greetings interrupted the usual early morning banter between administration staff. But it was short, slipping quickly into the mail room to grab the assignments and then retreating to the safety and anonymity of the writing lab. It was a sound plan until the school secretary blocked my escape. She was a tall, middle-aged woman with a robust figure and a raucous, infectious smile that matched her belly laugh. She wore a long floral dress with sleeves covering her shoulders. The only thing that changed daily was blue, red, or green. Her bouffant, afro-hair style crowned her round, beautiful face. A white frangipani flower rested provocatively upon her left ear, nestled among the wiry curls. Her smile beamed through full, soft lips no matter what time of the day. It was disarming, much like her personality. Nothing agitated her. Not even the Head of School could provoke a response in anger.

He certainly tried. But beneath that calm exterior was a person who was all business. That didn't mean there wasn't a little devil lurking in the devoutness of her beliefs.

'Professor, the Head of School wants to see you,' she said without looking up.

'Urgent, is it?'

'Isn't it always?'

'You're going to hell if he hears you say that.'

'I'm already there,' she smirked. 'Why do you think I am in church every Sunday?'

'Good point.'

'You'll be asking for forgiveness too if you don't drop by sometime this morning,' she said.

'I better not offend the gods. I've got to prepare for an eight o'clock class. How about ten?'

'He's got a meeting at 10.30 so don't be late. I'll book it in.'

'Keep Hell's fire and brimstone burning until then,' I offered, slipping into the mailroom.

A smile confirmed the time and opened the exit path and the pile of assignments. The pigeonhole was full. Thirty-eight was the count; each was dutifully typed and stapled with a course cover page. But three were missing. Two emails requested extensions, which were a tad late, but they'd given reasonable excuses to extend their deadline a couple of days. That left one more to make forty-one and the full complement for the class.

Nonetheless, that was a better-than-expected number for a first assignment. If effort could be equated with anything, hope might be rewarded today. But one certainty I've learned was that quantity rarely equates to quality.

With my bag and coffee, the added weight of expectation and assignments of the short commute to my office would make it awkward but manageable. It was a two-minute walk. There was a good chance of making it to safety without further disruption at this hour. Tucking the assignments securely under the same arm as the research articles had no impact on the coffee still locked in my left hand. There were always choices. Heading left would almost certainly lead to a meeting with the Head of School. That could wait until after class. Right, and back down the stairs it would be.

The arched pathway skewed right at the elbow of the building, dropping down a few steps to a purpose-built writing lab next to the newsroom. Students hung out or prepared stories for the weekly student newspaper and daily morning radio broadcasts. They were luckier than those in loftier places.

The lab was a large and well-equipped creative space. The room was free-floating, with moveable tables allowing the freedom to be malleable. Unlike the fixed rows of desks and chairs, it took students some time to feel comfortable in the new environment. They adapted and found ways to interact and create. That flexibility worked in other ways, too. The space had two entries. One is directly into the lab's writing area; the other at the opposite end of the building. That exit is a short corridor with three facing offices, exiting to an adjourning car park across from the small convenience store. Today might be one of those days to escape via the rear exit without being noticed. But that consideration was for later.

Unlocking the door to what seemed like a fishbowl looking out over the writing lab took a few adjustments of the bundle, bag, and coffee. It took a moment to find the office keys, and the latch clicked. A slight push with the shoulder, and it swung open. But the shift of weight unbalanced the assignments. A quick adjustment helped the falling pile find a home on the desk. A third sip of coffee would help with the sixty-two mostly irrelevant emails. Half were quickly deleted; the others were flagged for later. A call interrupted that allocation.

'Want to take the afternoon off and play hooky with me in the city?' Letitia asked.

'I have a class until ten, then a meeting, but I'm free after that,' I replied.

'Perfect, I'll pick you up in a taxi from the car park next to the corner store at twelve,' she said. 'We can grab some lunch when we get there.'

'Where are we going?'

'Wait and see.'

I stood up, kicked the chair back and slipped the phone into my front pocket. The chair rolled back to the pile of books and papers on the floor. They resisted momentarily, then no more. There was no need to re-stake the pile. Each one needed to be filed away anyway, so whether they were vertical or horizontal had little relevance to the clutter. There hadn't been time to organise the chaos. I grabbed my keys from the desk and gathered the course textbook, laptop, first round of writing responses in one arm, and coffee. It was more than a handful, so I was surprised by a smoother than anticipated departure. Navigating the door and the lock was a little trickier, and it closed with an audible clunk.

I exited through the writing lab into the covered corridor and set out for the rescheduled classroom. The campus map offering only a rudimentary description of the possible location. It would have been more helpful if all of the rooms were numbered, not just a few. A Resource Allocation and Scheduling email redirected me to G1.08, but was that a first-floor or ground-floor room?

No one was more pleased than me when several familiar faces popped out of the doorway to the room and waved me over. Several students offered to help, and I gladly handed over the papers to pass out as I headed for the computer and lectern. The projector flashed a quote on the large projection screen as students haggled for seats at the rear of the classroom.

'Coffee is more than just a drink; I it's something happening,' I read in bold Arial font. 'Not in a hip way. It's more like an event, a place to be, but not like a location, like somewhere within yourself. It gives you time, not hours or minutes, a chance to be yourself and have a second cup.'

It was attributed to Stein, but the language seemed a little too modern and hip for the 1930s. Nonetheless, its purpose was to grab the audience's attention, which might pull them from wandering thoughts and checking their phones. But most students took little notice, shuffled into their seats, and continued their conversations.

'Does anyone know who Gertrude Stein was?' I projected loudly to the back of the room, where students seemed oblivious to the class starting.

'Never met her, sir,' came one of the few male voices close to the rear exit door.

'I'm not surprised,' I said above the chorus of laughter. 'Stein's a famous writer, editor and art collector who lived more than eighty years ago, and she was a feminist when feminism was not so cool,' I explained.

I paused for a moment, scanning the room to put a face to the voice. There were two choices, but both had buried their faces into the desks to counter the lingering search.

'Can anyone give me a definition of feminism without looking it up on Google, please?' I continued.

'Women wanting equal rights,' a female student responded from the righthand side of the class, close to the door.

'Excellent,' I replied, casting a supportive glance to an auburn-haired girl staring directly at me. 'What else do we know about her?'

Their faces told me they didn't know, didn't care, or hadn't adequately woken.

'Ok, she was instrumental in helping and guiding the New Generation writers of the 1930s and 40s,' I continued without hesitating. 'Writers like Hemingway, Joyce and Barnes benefited greatly as friends, critics, and confidants. These were authors that changed the way we think of writing today.'

No one ventured a thought until the same auburn-haired student breached the uncomfortable silence.

'Wasn't Stein friends with Sylvia Beach, who published Joyce's first book?' came the same voice.

'Yes, she did,' I responded. '*Ulysses*, when no one else dared touch it. Like Joyce, Beach was a close friend and supporter of Stein, often visiting her at the bookstore on Rue de la Bûcherie.'

'I read that she did more for American-Britain diplomacy before and after her death than the buffoon appointed US ambassador. Is that true?'

'I've read a sign in her bookstore, Shakespeare & Company, that says just that,' I agreed. 'So, two powerful literary women guided a generation of writing titans, and these writers still have an impact today.'

Another check across the room at the young woman's face. It was as if she'd announced her arrival but remained nameless. I couldn't place her in class or remember seeing her before. That brief interaction could achieve more than I thought possible from the early exchange.

There was another more practical reason for choosing a female writer. Young women dominated class numbers, almost four to one. Though unplanned, the interchange grabbed their attention. But some were still struggling with the early rise. A reference to the film *Midnight in Paris* helped the reading-challenged film majors in the front row of the class. It was a harsh but accurate assessment, unfortunately. Several were the same students sitting at the coffee shop table earlier this morning.

Class wound to early end and departure, and I headed back to the office. But one student lingered and then joined me in lockstep. I glanced right and a familiar face smiled—the girl from the middle rows. Whatever she wanted, it would have to be quick. I needed to catch the taxi and I gestured for her to walk with me.

'Sir, sorry for bothering you, but can I ask a question?'

'I'm running a little late, so let's walk and talk if that's ok. Feedback or mark?'

'Neither sir.'

'What's your name?' I interrupted.

'Sorry, Katherine, with a K. Katherine Brooks. People call me Kat, and I'm a second-year student, the one who talks too much in class.'

'Jack Graham, with a D and an R,' I smiled. 'The one who likes you talking too much in class. We need more of that, so please don't apologise and don't stop.'

'Yes, sir.'

'So, there's no mark because I wanted you to focus on re-writing your sample without worrying about that aspect. Students focus too much on the mark. What I want to see is you working on your craft. You can re-submit it later, and you'll be given a grade. Ok?'

'Sir, I haven't submitted yet,' she said.

'So, you're forty-one,' I added.

Kat stared at me, trying to determine what the number meant, and she decided it wasn't necessary to know.

'Sorry, I was sick the first couple of weeks. That's why I haven't been to class and submitted the assignment. But my question is more of a query. I'm struggling with another writing task. Not for this course. It's an in-class exercise we must do, and to be honest, it scares the fuck out of me. Sorry for the language. I don't think I can write on command.'

'That'll take a little longer than we have right now,' I said as we approached the writing lab entrance and a Head of School meeting I was already late for. 'I'm happy to meet with you later in the week. Can you come by the lab on Wednesday or Thursday? Is that too late?'

'No, no, that's perfect. I have plenty of time, and the test's not until the week after next. When are your office hours?'

'Open door. I'm available when I'm there, and it's open.'

'Thank you, sir. Much appreciated.'

'Make sure you get that assignment to me in the next couple of days.'

CHAPTER 5

I had little to do besides unloading the laptop before heading upstairs to the meeting. Despite the promise to arrive at ten, the short exchange with Kat had pushed that arrival back ten minutes. I'd have to live with the delay. Besides, the longer the meeting, the less enjoyable it would be for the person under discussion. I had almost made it to the office as he rounded the elbow of the corridor before a voice interrupted my progress.

'Hold up,' the Head of the School yelled. 'Running a bit late.'

'All good. I'm a little late myself.'

'Class or students?'

'Both.'

Meetings with the Head of School were much like fly fishing. You were unsure whether you were the angler, the lure, or the fish. He was unpredictable, depending on his mood. Undoubtedly, he was a learned man, far more worldly than other locals. A Master's degree from the United States and a doctorate from a Melbourne-based university, the name of which escaped me presently. It wasn't necessary, knowing I'd be soon reminded of it. That was part of his mannerism, embedding himself in every conversation no matter the topic or length of interaction. And he was always the hero. Everything else about him seemed average, except for his deceptive charm.

Maybe that was his secret weapon. One intended to disarm. It hid a rational, strategic and discerning political animal, skills honed over years of playing a dangerous game; one made for the type of animal he'd become. There were always winners and losers, but not him. Each move was calculated. He'd repeatedly recalled his most harrowing time during one coup, surviving on his wits as he evaded police and inevitable arrest by minutes. He held up first in his office and then at a friend's house for nearly a month to avoid the search. Outside, the political turmoil rolled over the island like a tropical thunderstorm and on to its predictable end. And his hero status grew if only in the tales he told ad nauseam to those who'd listen and others who'd feign interest in the hope of escaping the predictable ending.

I followed him into the office and sat down. On the desk were piles of papers, an open laptop and a polished wooden name plate that read 'Professor Ravi Mishra.'

'What's the update on our misfortunate friend,' Ravi said without looking up.

'It'll go to dispute as you predicted.'

'If we are going to make this program world-class, we must clean house.'

'Agree, but that's not going to happen without a fight. If I were him, I'd do the same if it meant keeping my job.'

'That's not going to happen, and we need to ensure it doesn't.'

'We've presented a strong case for his dismissal,' I said. 'That action is now before the independent committee to decide, which should happen in a week, as HR informed me yesterday.'

'Is there anything more we can do?'

'Not from the advice of HR.'

'Well, we will see then, won't we?'

It seemed the lecturer's fate was no longer in the hands of the committee to hear his plea and remain at the university passed his current contract. Influence and decision-making aside, he'd contributed to his demise long before next week's meeting. On arrival, one of the first tasks assigned to me was to get the lecturer on track and finish his doctoral thesis. It was clear that he'd be gone if he didn't progress.

Publish or perish is the academic mantra. He was about to find out the ugly truth behind that statement. He either didn't take that threat seriously or relied on the system that had gotten him this far.

After two months, several meetings and no progress, the thesis remained mired in disorganisation and confusion. It wasn't going to pass the review process. But that wasn't his only problem. He was a foreigner with only working rights, not to mention the mounting pressure from a growing chorus of student complaints, which had become louder by the day. Frustrated students unleashed on the once favoured lecturer. Perhaps it was said best by Napoleon, that glory is fleeting, obscurity is forever. He was about to find out the harsh reality of the latter.

Ravi had called for an official report on his progress, and the purge began. A five-page assessment concluded he'd made no significant progress on his doctorate, and there was evidence supporting the student complaints. It didn't leave much room for a response. The Head of School didn't hesitate about the lecturer's future. At one level, you could feel sympathy for him. But he'd committed academic suicide by not delivering on the publishing and qualifications.

After the meeting, I hurried past the writing lab and headed for the car park. A large blue and white Toyota taxi hummed patiently in a no-standing, handicapped zone. Hazard lights flashed a shadowy excuse for its morally bankrupt resting place. Then, a horn blasted across the blackened bitumen space. I looked into the car, but seeing through the window's reflection was impossible. I opened the door, and Letitia waved me inside. She wore black jeans, a loose-fitting black T-shirt and a baseball cap with her ponytail jutting above the adjustment strap. Her eyes lit up as I slid into the backseat and closed the door with the customary thud of a Toyota Crown.

The taxi pulled up outside the OneRepublic coffee shop, a place as familiar as any on the island. It has become an oasis of peace away from the heat and a much-needed break from work. The coffee was strong, and the snacks were sweet. But an old favourite beckoned on most occasions. A grilled ham and cheese sandwich was comfort food, a reminder of home that made life a little more palatable.

'One of my Zen places,' I said, following Letitia into the coffee shop. 'A peaceful sanctuary from the outside world.'

'Let's grab the seat in the corner,' she said, pointing to the red velvet chairs facing the road and petrol station. 'What would you like?' I asked.

'Iced mocha.'

I waited in line to order and then returned to the table where Letitia sat, staring out towards the service station across the road, watching the occasional passers-by.

'Can I ask you a personal question?' I said as I sat down into the welcoming embrace of the plush comfort.

'Sure,' she said.

'What colour is that nail polish?' I said, gently touching her hand resting idly on her knee.

'You want to know the colour?' She responded with a wry smile.

'Of course.'

'Cobalt Blue. Do you like it?'

'It's a bold choice,' I responded.

'I felt like celebrating.'

'What are you celebrating exactly?'

'You, actually.'

'Me, what did I do?'

'You came back,' Letitia said. 'Everyone was so excited when we heard you were arriving.'

'Good news travels fast,' I responded.

'Very good news, and none travelled faster for me.'

'Are you flirting with me?'

'Maybe.'

'You know we would never work, you and me.'

'Why is that?'

'You're way too smart and beautiful, and I need to be the beautiful one in the relationship.'

Letitia's smile lit a fire on her cheeks. It may have been an old smile, but it seemed fresh and full of possibility today, as though it had little positive nurturing until now.

I looked down and noticed her coffee cup partially hid a small stack of stapled A4 papers on the table. I could make out only a few words of the title and her name at the bottom of the page, which piqued my interest.

'Have you published your research?'

'That's even more personal than the last question,' she said. 'No, I haven't published any of my writing.'

'Why not?'

'I just don't feel comfortable with people reading what I write.'

'Why don't you feel comfortable?'

'Every person I know has told me that local women don't make it in academia.'

'That's nonsense,' I said. 'What's being a woman got to do with it?'

'If you've noticed, men here live privileged lives. At every meeting, there's a line-up of men. Every time you speak, they stare at you. I'm either ignored, interrupted, or dismissed, and that's a big deterrent.'

'What about the two Deputy Vice-Chancellors, both women.'

'Foreigners,' she responded. 'They get a pass because the university wants their experience and reputation. When people say so often that you won't make it, you start believing them.'

'You know, when I was young, people said the same thing to me,' I responded.

'Really?' Letitia responded in a disbelieving tone.

'When your father tells you that you'll be nothing, be no one, it's a huge blow. So, I understand that feeling somewhat.'

'How did you move on?'

'I felt something more was out there for me, drawing me to an unknown future. You never know what lies ahead.'

'I feel I am destined for more than people here think I can become,' Letitia said. 'But I'm not sure I have what it takes.'

'Look around you,' I said. 'Everyone here has a gift, a talent. Some may not know what that gift or talent is just yet. But everyone is talented in some way or another. But having something to say and finding a way to say it so people listen is another thing. There are plenty of people with nothing to say. Do you have something to say, Letitia?'

'I'm not sure, maybe.'

'Either you do, or you don't. Which one is it?'

'I'm not sure I can write like you.'

'You don't have to write like me,' I responded. 'You just gotta write and trust the process. Among all the nonsense that passes as truth, we are here on this planet to say something people want to hear. You understand what I'm saying?'

'Yeah, I understand,' Letitia said. 'I don't believe it, but I understand it.'

'I think you believe it a little bit. The alternative is just too painful. One thing that makes academia bearable is that you can wrap yourself in the blanket of anonymity, and submitting your work under blind review is a liberating experience.'

'The blind leading the blind,' she quipped.

'Yeah, something like that,' I agreed. 'Remember one important thing. Go after what you want, and don't let anyone say or do anything that stops you from achieving your goals. Remember, if it's not a wet dream, it's just foreplay. All the rest is corridor gossip and coffee-house bullshit.'

'Remind me not to talk about writing with you again,' Letitia said with an agreeable smile.

For the first time in a week, that comfortable feeling returned. Just a few more days, and hopefully, they'd pass smoothly. I'd formed an escape plan to the other side of the island where people could be anonymous, if only for a short time. I considered hiring a car, but Queens Road offered much more than a way to get to the other side. It stretched along the southwestern side of the big island, and its beauty was as if Monet had pleaded with God to create a vista worthy of the celestial artist's talents. In truth, the beaches were far superior to those at the resorts. But there was no better place to land if you yearned for privacy and well-prepared alchemy from the pool bar.

'I've booked a room at a resort for my birthday,' I said. 'Would you like to celebrate with me, away from here and prying eyes?'

'Yes, more than anything,' Letitia responded.

CHAPTER 6

'Everyone aboard,' the bus driver yelled through the open door of the tourist shop just thirty minutes into the four-hour ride.

'We gotta go,' I said.

'No, we've got another fifteen minutes at least,' Letitia responded. 'Don't worry. They're not going to leave us behind. It'd be bad for business to leave a foreigner stranded here. Besides, the driver and his friend are chatting with their cousin outside. They'll be at it a while longer.'

'Right,' I responded, staring into the car park. 'Do you know them?'

'Which shirt do you like?' Letitia said, ignoring my questions and waving blue, green and white floral shirts like fluttering flags on a flagpole from across the aisles crowded with cheap Chinese-made clothes.

'How do you know they're cousins?' I persisted.

'Wouldn't have stopped here if they weren't, and the way they talk to each other, they're either brothers or cousins. I think they're cousins, as they don't look much alike. Not the same father.'

The large bus driver dominated the discussion, laughing loudly at the shorter, leaner cousin who tried to chime into the conversation only to be shut down mid-response. The call on them being cousins seemed a solid assessment, though there was no way to know what they were saying in the local dialect. The lack of understanding did not impact how entertaining the conversation was as they relentlessly teased and prodded one another.

'Which size and colour?' Letitia said, checking again.

'Um, the white one, I think. Medium. Yes, that one!'

Out of the bus's window, the island side view of the rugged, heavily forested mountain ranges circled into a singular blur as the vehicle swept along the sharp bends and curves of the coastline. To the East, the white, coral coastline presented a picture-perfect poster shot an hour into the winding journey along Queens Road. Nestled amongst the extended bays and white beaches rested five-star resorts and budget bungalows vying for small pockets of usable land and pristine beaches. The kind families favoured. It wouldn't have been difficult to imagine stepping off the bus and into any one of the pool-side villas for a long weekend. But that wasn't the plan. Putting some distance between home and destiny meant the secluded Radisson Blu Resort.

When the bus stopped for each waving passenger and the scheduled resorts, the trip stretched past the afternoon arrival time and into the early evening. The bus arrived just in time to catch the last service at the restaurant before heading to the room exhausted.

CHAPTER 7

Waking up at 3am is no fun when you're alone, but even more so when you're not. Letitia's slow breathing and warm body curled perfectly within a tight embrace. But that wasn't enough to return to sleep. By 4.30am, restlessness replaced the temptation to wake her. A T-shirt and shorts cut the coolness of the air-conditioned room but were perfect for the still-humid night air. A last-minute change of room had given us quick access to the barely lit path running westward along the shoreline.

My pace matched the hushed splashes of waves as they ended their journey, only to retreat silently back into the bay. The walkway curved crescent-like to the shoreline, with smaller access paths spilling off one after the other to each of the increasingly more expensive and exclusive resorts and villas. As the night bled into early morning, the walkway lamps flickered their retreat. The moment between nightfall and daybreak creates an eerie, strangely comforting silence. It erases all that has come before it and, with it, the promise of something new, better.

I sat down on the edge of the sand. The thin strip of grass became a soft landing to watch that vivid scene unfold. Taking in a sunrise never loses its beauty, emerging light shifting from orange to purple hues, haphazardly splashed against the still semi-dark skyline. That half-life is neither night nor day. But those chaotic brush strokes flickered and then began fading from the sky.

A flick of the feet discarded the thongs, and my toes squirrelled deep into the cool, moist sand. It was twenty minutes or maybe longer since leaving the room. I didn't know, didn't rightly care. The sound of footsteps jolted me away from the serene picture. But there was no need to look. Her presence filled the air like the scent of the first rain. And she came to me like a summer breeze, a warmth as soft as your eyes could be in the morning light. I wanted to feel her in my arms again as she moved closer.

Letitia veered off the pathway for the grass and sand. The red and yellow wrap-around floral dress synchronised movement to the light breeze. A heavier gust caught the small, untethered flap, unfurling the soft cotton print and exposing her inner thigh. She looked down but didn't cover up.

'There's nothing quite so beautiful, is there?' she said, looking to the horizon.

There was no need to reply. She was right, but I wasn't focusing on the horizon. The light cradled her face with a soft, radiant embrace. It cast across the bridge of her nose and caught the far-side cheek; Rembrandt would have approved. It was a picture-perfect moment that could be retrieved at my time from my memory palace.

'I could think of one or two things,' I responded.

Letitia smiled. It was unclear as to whether it was flirtation or seduction or whether it even mattered. It was more than just an idle statement. My glances took in her beauty, with her gentle curves reminding me of the spell I was under, one I gratefully accepted. It was beautiful to gaze upon someone and feel as though a future was possible with that person. It was a future filled with happiness, contentment, and, most of all, love. Things that had escaped me long ago and seemed lost forever.

'I woke up, and you weren't there,' she said, quickly closing the short distance from the path to the sand and sitting down beside me.

The incoming tide covered our feet in ankle-deep water.

'I remembered you were saying how much you loved the water, so I kept walking until I saw you.'

'It calms and clears my mind.'

The light floral fragrance pulled my attention away from the vista laid out before me. It did so not in a bold way but delicately, as though the dress itself emitted the floral notes. It reminded me of something pleasant and comforting. I remembered science classes with Ms Landon, a blonde Dane by birth and beauty by design. For some, the meeting of God and science may seem strange bedfellows. But God was on point. With a sweep of blonde hair tucked neatly behind her ear until it fell back, she leaned across the lab benches to explain a chemical reaction and those tight-fitting white tops and hugging, thigh-length skirts, far too much stimulation for a teenage boy. By the second day, I'd changed my mind about science, but it was anatomy that filled my thoughts more than chemistry. I'd memorised every curve and every edge. If I'd paid more attention in class, it might have helped me understand the Petri dish of emotions coursing through my brain now and other less thoughtful organs.

We both sat silently at first, watching the last remnants of the light show unfold in the distance as the heat and humidity began to rise in synchronicity with the sun. It might have been a few minutes or longer before either said a word, and we were unconcerned about the comfortable silence or time.

Only the mild throttle of a jet ski, spluttering slowly out to a yacht anchored offshore, cut the quiet.

'Some people call me Letitia,' she said finally. 'Others call me Leti.'

'Which do you prefer?' I responded.

'I think we're more than friends after last night. So, either one is fine with me. I *do* love how you say, Letitia.'

'How's that?'

'It's more than a word. It's like you breathe life into it. Does that make sense?'

'There's that writer in there.'

What they say about names indeed means more than their form. Sometimes, it shows where you come from; others about where you've been and how you got there. I wasn't always Jack, and I didn't want to follow in the same footsteps as my father. Of course, it's never as simple as a matter of choice. Sometimes, the reasons run much deeper.

'I'm not sure where Letitia comes from. My aunt named me. But I know my middle name Devi means princess in Hindi.'

'Seems appropriate.'

'What does that mean?'

'Letitia is the name of a Saint.'

'You're making this up!'

'No, it's true. St. Letitia was a Spanish deity who spread blessings to Corsica and England.'

'Really? How do you know this? Wait, why did I even say that? What do they say about idle hands?'

'More like busy fingers.'

'Googled it, huh?' She responded. 'Do you do that with all the girls you meet?'

'What's that?'

'Sweep them off their feet with random facts?'

'Not all, just the beautiful ones,' I said without looking up to see her reaction. 'Not so many of those in my travels.'

'Sweet talker,' she replied. 'Not sure how true it is, but sounds pretty interesting?'

'I can attest interesting is better than true, don't you think? And there's even more. Did you know she was a virgin martyr?'

'A virgin, well I think that's where St. Letitia and I take different paths,' she said with a slight smirk.

'You and I both,' I agreed. 'But it doesn't diminish the blessing you've brought to my life.'

'There you go again, all nice and sweet like.'

It was as though she hadn't heard a compliment in quite a while. She seemed suspicious of the generosity, or was it simply curiosity of the altruism? That same pathology had lingered long and large in my life, one littered with such errors in judgment. Wanting to do the right thing can end in self-harm. Resulting trauma can do the same, producing a desperate need to help people who exploit the situation repeatedly. I'd let it happen. But to say I deserved the existential consequences of such actions would be far too harsh a call. One thing's for sure, I knew that had to change.

'Jack, I have to tell you something. You'll not be happy when I do, but I must say it. I'm unsure how, and I've thought long and hard about it and struggled.'

'It sounds serious. Tell me please.'

'I haven't been completely truthful with you,' Letitia said, pausing. 'I even considered not coming this weekend and emailing you, but I couldn't do that, not to you.'

All the playfulness had gone from her voice. It was serious, and I listened.

'Please forgive me, I'm married!' she blurted out. 'I'm so sorry. I wanted to tell you before now.'

Letitia rocked back, and her face collapsed into her hands. Expecting the worst was the least she thought would happen, and each second of silence contributed to her possible fate.

'Didn't work out, huh?' I said.

'You knew?'

'No, but I suspected something wasn't right. The texting, rushing off after boxing.'

'You're not angry?'

'Why would I be angry? I'm pleased you told me what was going on. I was confused for some time but hoped you'd trust me.'

'I'm stunned, to be honest.'

'You had your reasons for not telling me,' I said. 'I don't know what is happening, but I can tell it's serious and affecting your life. You're not happy, and I'm here for you, and I just want you to know that.'

'I wasn't expecting this.'

I could have been angry, and no one would have judged me for it. After all, it didn't seem casual; maybe it was, and I'd misread the situation. But Letitia hadn't walked away.

'My marriage could have worked,' Letitia responded. 'We were good together for a long time. Nothing was too much, and everything else too little. We were in love. After we were married, we moved in with his family over in the West. They needed him to work on the farm after his father fell ill. So, we moved. It was the right thing to do.'

Sugar cane farming is hard work no matter where it grows. I had watched generations of farmers toil harder than most for little return. Droughts and floods tempered the occasional good years when the rains held off and the harvest reaped bumper crops and reasonable prices for a much sought-after commodity. Days of toil were long and nights even longer. Before sunrise, my father would rise and ride the old grey Massey Ferguson tractor, ploughing the fields with one weak headlight. That little warhorse never faltered, no matter the heat and dust. By 7am, he'd swapped the fine dust of the fields for even finer metals of the shipbuilding yards. Forty years with no protection hardened the lungs and shortened his life. Returning from overseas revealed a once strong, proud man withered to the bone. Each breath sounded like a death rattle. It was a blessing when his heart gave way, saving him from a painful and fearful end as he would have gasped for life with every breath.

'I thought I could help, but it became a nightmare,' she continued. 'I cooked and cleaned for the family, up at sunrise and last to sleep. They treated me like a servant. *Do this, don't do that.* They'd yell orders at me and complain when things weren't done the right way, their way. I complained, but he wouldn't listen. He'd just say wives do what they're told. I couldn't believe what I was hearing. I cried every night and prayed for it to stop. I told my mother what was happening. I was desperate. She said if it's that bad, leave, go back home.'

Tears streamed down her cheek. I tried to comfort her, placing a hand on her shoulder and reassuring her with slow, comforting strokes.

'Mother was right,' she said. 'My husband returned home, apologetic and thoughtful. I hoped it would be like it was, but it was not the answer, far from it for a while, it seemed like old times. We were happy, but it didn't last. Little things made him angry. He swapped nights at home for drinking with his friends, and I joined in. We drank too much and partied too hard. I could stay out all night, but he wanted to go home. He said I shouldn't be out without him. He got angrier and angrier. We talked less, and argued more.'

She took a deep breath and exhaled her pain. I waited. If I said something now, it wouldn't make it any easier for her. So, I let her breathe and collect herself.

'Then I fell pregnant. I stopped drinking, but he didn't.'

'Didn't or couldn't?' I asked.

'What's the difference?'

'Not much, I guess.'

'That's when it got worse. He said it wasn't his baby. He said I'd been sleeping with other men. I couldn't convince him. The stress became too much, and I started bleeding. I was so scared. He didn't care. I think he wanted it gone. The doctor said I had to rest without stress, and everything would be ok; the baby would be ok. My husband suggested we go back to live with his family again. That wasn't an option. There was no rest there, no peace, more stress. Besides, I'd started teaching again with reduced hours. We needed the money. I started to feel better about myself, like I was doing something good, making a difference and not disappointing anyone. Then, one day, I felt sharp pangs.'

'I lost the baby that night. I felt empty, hollow,' she said.

'I'm so sorry.' I uttered what seemed useless words.

I wanted to take away the pain. But what do you say to someone you so desperately want to help, to comfort but can't, no matter what you say or do?

'Things changed. He changed. I hadn't just lost a baby; I'd lost him. I shouldn't be loved if I weren't good enough to carry his child. It made no sense, but his mood darkened. I tried to comfort and help him through it, but couldn't. I felt like I'd failed him again. I needed something positive in my life. A change of direction, so I started studying. I loved it: the research, the teaching, the students, all of it. Then I started working with women at the crisis centre.'

'The purple one down on Gordon Street,' I replied.

'Yes, that god-awful coloured building. But the centre does amazing work with women affected by domestic violence. They offer support, advice, and safety. But that just made him angrier. If women did as they were told, they wouldn't have a problem, he'd say. That wasn't aimed at them but me. I'd changed and become more independent. He couldn't accept that, wouldn't accept it. I couldn't be what he wanted, and I eventually learned to be ok with that.'

Exhausted or relieved, maybe both, she stopped talking. It's easy to sympathise but much more difficult to empathise. There was no way of knowing what she'd sacrificed.

'There's a saying that goes something like, what the caterpillar sees as the end of the world, the butterfly sees a new beginning,' I said, hoping it would mean something to her. 'Maybe education is your cocoon. It certainly changed my life. The more I studied, the more I felt a purpose. I'd found safety there, but it came at a cost. Like you, I couldn't relate to those around me as it filled and overwhelmed the void. I was consumed by it. I thrived in this new world. For a long time, I thought I'd found what I'd been searching for, a haven.'

Like Letitia's moment of truth, this one would also be important. Only the waves rolling in and out filled the silence.

'I sense a big but coming,' she said.

'Indeed,' I said. 'She's a demanding mistress, that one. The more I gave to her, the more she demanded. She was insatiable. I couldn't slow down. If I did, I thought I'd lose whatever this thing was that made me so good at it. One publication became two, then ten. They rolled effortlessly into the spotlight. Everything was so easy. I bounced from Singapore to the States. It was a way to test myself against the best, and the opportunity came. I grabbed it with both hands. I hit the tenure track running. Five years to full professor, and I had everything I wanted.'

'I can't even imagine what that would be like,' she said. 'For me, that seems impossible.'

'I'd thought that too,' I replied. 'It was momentum I couldn't stop even if I wanted to. One opportunity created another. Without realising it, my career moved forward with ruthless determination, no matter the cost to those around me. It was exhilarating. I'd finally found a home where I excelled. The adoration was addictive. I'd look around the room in meetings, sitting at the same table with the best minds in the world. Nothing could stop me. Some days, I might have been as good as I thought I was. I loved every minute: the research, the writing, the recognition. I wasn't just good at something. I was the best.'

A voice inside screamed silently, *shut the fuck up*! Erecting walls and compartmentalising my life ruthlessly for so long, and here I was letting her in. Each move I'd made since a child was based on survival, and it had worked. With practice came perfection. She sensed my reluctance to continue, holding my hand and gently squeezing it.

'Trust me,' she said. 'Let's walk back to the resort and grab some breakfast.'

I stopped speaking as we made our way back along the path. But curiosity got the better of her.

'Why are you here?' she asked.

'What do you mean?'

'You had it all,' she said. 'What happened in the US?'

'I fucked it up. Maybe I wanted it too much, and when it all happened, I couldn't balance work and family between what was important and what was just bullshit. My marriage broke down, and everything collapsed. I collapsed. I wanted to take time out and fix it, but the pressure to stay on the never-ending academic treadmill was too much. Publish or perish, they say. I didn't realise that even then, it was too much, too late. I'd already lost what was important. I'd forgotten the most important thing: enjoy the moment and saviour it with those who matter.'

She kindly waited for my atonement to move past that moment before I pushed the conversation in a new direction.

'You know the worst time of the day is three in the morning,' I said. 'I wake up and start listing all the people, places and things that could have been done differently. It's like a broken fucking record.'

We passed a small white church, and the conversation turned to confession. I barely knew this person, but I wanted so desperately to trust her, let her in, and give her a chance to know me. There it was again, that lingering enigma of hope, tantalisingly close. I hoped she wouldn't be disappointed in my failings. She sensed how uncomfortable I felt and provided an out.

'I saw you walking to the office with a woman the other day. Is she on your list?'

'No.'

'She's beautiful,' Letitia said.

'You look alright, too,' I responded nonchalantly.

She laughed. It was not an uncomfortable laugh out of politeness but honest and true. When you hear both, you can tell the difference.

'Thank you,' she said. 'What about your students? Are they on your list?'

'Some of them. I worry I'm too hard on them. But by five o'clock I've decided it's ok. They need to know what writing for a living is like.'

The laugh this time was different, muffled but there.

'Then there's you,' I said.

'I'm on the list?'

'Yeah, it's a pretty fucking long list. No wonder I can't sleep.'

'Why are you thinking about me at 3am?'

'I just think you and I are the same,' I said.

'Really, how so?'

'We're both searching for something to give our lives meaning. Tell me, what is the thing you yearn for the most?'

'Freedom,' she said without hesitating.

'For me, it's redemption,' I responded. 'That's a kind of freedom, isn't it? Freedom from your past mistakes.'

No more was said. Letitia wrapped her arms around my waist and pulled me into her body. Her forehead snuggled into my shoulder as my arms surrounded her, and a light kiss caressed her forehead. Within a few steps, she moved slightly away and interlocked her fingers with mine, which felt comfortable and right.

'All this fresh air is making me hungry,' I said. 'The buffet looks amazing.'

'Sure,' she said hesitantly.

'You must be hungry. You barely ate last night.'

'No, it's not that. It doesn't matter.'

'What is it?'

'It doesn't matter. Let's go.'

Arriving at the breakfast buffet at 6am is the best time. Fewer people and the food is fresh. We surveyed the dishes on a long table to the left of the service area. Letitia took a plate and headed for the vegetarian section. I stayed in line for the bacon and eggs, along with several couples and a family. She filled her plate quickly.

Letitia passed by me and reached out to touch my arm. She gestured to a table on the other side of the dining area where no one was sitting. Perhaps she was worried someone might recognise her, or she simply liked a quieter area away from the families and kids. But I saw most of the staff and the family tracking her to the other side of the room. I watched her settle at the table as I shuffled forward in line. The server filled the plate with bacon, eggs, toast, and beans. I looked eagerly toward the coffee area to see if they'd placed a fresh pot. They hadn't, but they would if requested.

'How's the breakfast?' I asked, sitting down next to her.

'It's good. There's quite a good spread.'

But every time she took a mouthful, there was a nervous glance around the room as more families and couples entered the dining area.

'Worried someone might know you?'

'No,' she responded.

'You keep looking around the room,' I said, turning to see what she was looking at.

'It's not that. It's how people look at us.'

'What do you mean? No one is looking at *us*. They're looking at me.'

'People think I'm a prostitute because I'm with you and not wearing a ring doesn't help.'

'And I'm a foreigner, so you must be, right,' I said.

'Yes.'

'They'd be even more judgmental if they knew what we did last night and what I'm thinking of doing it again right now,' I quipped.

The wink was quick, but she noticed it, and it relaxed her.

'I'm done,' she said as she discarded the knife and fork, grabbed my hand, and pulled me toward the exit.

The sudden departure might have attracted attention if it wasn't for the refilling of the buffet breakfast tables. Finishing off the almost cold bacon and runny scrambled eggs wasn't even a consideration, nor was the coffee. The off-menu service was much more enjoyable. Whatever moral mischievousness was committed last night had two very willing accomplices. The key had barely clicked free as we fell into the room. The door crashed against the wall and then slammed shut. If that were the loudest sound coming from the room in the next hour, then that'd be ok with the neighbours.

'Hey, we need to shower and go if we're going to catch the afternoon bus,' she whispered.

'Sorry. I fell asleep?'

'Worn out, huh? Let's go. I packed everything and showered. We've got fifteen minutes before the bus goes.'

'So, we've got 30 minutes.'

'Wouldn't it be good if it was that simple? No, departures run on time.'

CHAPTER 8

The bus trip back passed slowly. We talked about travelling abroad, maybe Paris, and strolling along the Left Bank. Barcelona was a possibility. The Gothic centre was always a treat, with its cobblestone side streets filled with small boutique shops. She wanted the world, and I wanted her. But there was no time for that.

The bus slipped through one village after another, briefly stopping to drop off and pick up passengers before winding its way back along the white coral coastline. The small coves passed like dotted lines on the highway; too many to count, too fast to see much difference. Children ran and swam in the shallows.

'What's so interesting out the window?' Letitia asked.

'I don't see anyone looking after the kids,' I responded, pointing to a group of maybe eight or ten children chasing each other through shallow waters.

'No need,' she said.

'Don't their parents worry?'

'They're born waterproof. Most swim before they walk and don't venture far from shallows, with no large waves or rips. The reef offers a protective cocoon. So, no supervision required.'

'Makes sense, I guess!'

Arriving at Holiday Inn was a brief grab-and-go with taxis lining up inside the hotel car park and along the road. We settled comfortably into the conversation for the twenty-minute trip back to the apartment. The car sped along the foreshore. It wasn't the shortest way home, but a few extra minutes counted as the car turned onto the main road and passed quickly by the university, veering off toward Fletcher Road and the airport. I leaned across the seat.

'Want to come up?' I whispered. 'Stay the night.'

'I can't,' she said. 'I need to organise a class for tomorrow. Hope that's ok.'

It wasn't. But three days and an extra night wouldn't appease my desire now or ever, and I didn't know what would have. She told the driver to go on to Vatuwaqa. The taxi slipped by the encampment and crunched across the iron bridge. Everything changed when it left the bridge — houses, people, the future.

'Can you pull over at the corner store,' Letitia asked. 'I need to grab a couple of things.'

'Ok,' said the driver. 'But your friend needs to go with you. I don't like the look of those boys over there.'

To the left of the store and fifty metres from the taxi, four teenagers looked up—each one aimless and shirtless, with lean, muscular bodies. One mouthed an inaudible comment. The others laughed and stood up to join their friend. That made the taxi driver nervous. I didn't think much of it, but the driver registered the threat. Letitia didn't hesitate and grabbed my hand, pulling me out of the taxi.

'Better to be safe,' she said as they quickly managed the three steps that separated them from the store's safety.

If we'd been listening, they would have heard the doors lock to secure the taxi from the approaching crew. I expected to see the four teenagers as we exited the doorway. Instead, the driver leaned against one of the old wooden pylons that stopped the rusted tin roof from tumbling down. He casually twirled an old cricket bat in his left hand, caressed red by more than a few glancing blows. The four stood steadfast a few metres away, unsure whether to advance or retreat. The leader turned, and the others followed in lockstep. One of the men glanced back as we slipped into the protective skin of the taxi.

'I never leave home without it,' the driver said as he stowed the willow under the bench seat for safekeeping and easy access.

'Looks like you've had some experience with that,' I said.

'A few innings,' he responded. 'Enough to know what a good piece of wood and a solid swing can do.'

The brakes squealed their displeasure as the taxi pulled up next to the grassed curb opposite the back entrance to Letitia's house.

'I'm not going to kiss you goodbye,' she said. 'Don't want the neighbours discussing me more than they already do. I just wanted you to know I had an amazing time. Hope you enjoyed your birthday present.'

My smile acknowledged the night before and the morning after. She opened the door and stepped onto the footpath leading to the house. The driver pulled a lever, and the back door closed with a thud. Old cars make solid noises. I tapped the driver on the shoulder and gestured to lower the window. The small motor whirred its gradual decline until it stopped halfway.

'Hey,' I called out through the window.

'Don't give me that look,' she said without stopping or turning around.

'What look?'

'That one!'

'It's the only one I've got.'

'You have my number,' she responded.

'Alright!'

Her fingernails flashed a brilliant blue as she waved goodbye. I watched as she walked towards the open gate. I slid across the leather seat as the driver pressed the button on the dashboard, and the window squeaked its return. The car accelerated around the corner and toward Beach Road and the apartment.

'Maybe I fucked that up,' I mumbled to the world flashing by.

'Nah,' the taxi driver said. 'You did just fine.'

PART THREE

CHAPTER 9

A knock on the glass door was barely audible, a light touch to announce, not annoy. At least, that's what it seemed like. A familiar face peered through the wide glass window panel. Kat's striking green eyes flashed a pleading request to enter. It must be important because I'd made my open-door policy clear. But there was no way of hiding from anyone in the writing lab, with the sizeable window offering a panoptic view into the creative space. I felt like a goldfish as the pleading eyes sought divine intervention or at least a measure of forgiveness. It might take a healthy portion of both. A tilt of the head released Kat from her momentary penance. She pushed the door open and stood in the doorway, uncommitted to a full entry.

'Come in,' I said without looking up from my keyboard. 'Take a seat wherever you can find one.'

'Good morning, Professor,' Kat responded as she looked around the cluttered room to find a place to land.

There wasn't one. Kat found the chairs piled with papers and books. I smiled at her mild discomfort, but she didn't notice.

'You can put those on the floor,' I said, pointing to the chair closest to the door.

Kat gathered the books and tried to arrange them carefully, but that proved far more challenging than I'd thought. The pile swayed left, then tilted right, finally giving way and toppling to the floor.

'Don't worry about it,' I said, easing her concern. 'I need to find a place for them anyway.'

If she wasn't nervous to start with, she certainly was now. So often, what we think is urgent is a matter of perspective. Hopefully, the interruption was significant and not simply a whim or, worse, lousy time management. She surveyed the rows of textbooks and novels arranged haphazardly on the lone grey steel bookshelf towering above her.

'You've read all these books?' she said nervously.

'No, I just keep them to impress students. How did I do?'

'Those on the top row are not my preference,' she said, pointing to the academic texts. 'These here, though, are much more to my liking.'

'You prefer the classics?'

'Yes, but not specifically those, though I've read Hemingway and Orwell. I liked *Animal Farm* more than the others. *Down and Out in Paris and London* painted a grim picture of places and time, but it made me want to visit nonetheless.'

'Stark realism,' I responded, pointing to the lower sections of the bookshelves. 'Just below those is the four-volume set of Orwell's letters and short articles. Quite an insight into the places and people he recreated.'

There was something about her that I liked immediately. Our first meeting a few days earlier had been brief, but there was an air of confidence usually vacant in young islanders. She was born into island life but was not from the islands. There were obvious signs of European influence not just in her Caucasian features but her mannerisms. Cascading auburn locks curled comfortably to the shoulder, framing her translucent, freckled skin. She could easily be mistaken for an Irish lass if it wasn't for the slight accent or lack of one.

'What did you like about their work?' I asked.

'Anything biographical or autobiographical is interesting,' she responded. 'Those with a little truth but well written. I'm not opposed to a well-constructed lie if it is interesting and true to the writer and the story.'

'But how do you know what is true and what is not?' I responded.

'I don't think it matters. Maybe that's the most interesting part, trying to find out which one.'

'Getting the balance is the challenge, do you agree?'

'The last thing I want is to be complicit to a lie,' Kat said. 'If a writer lets me in on the secret from the start and entices me for the ride, then I am in for the journey.'

'So fanciful and believable can reside in the same universe?' I said.

'I don't see them as opposites, more composites,' she responded. 'The story can be fanciful, almost impossible, but the characters must be believable, true to their experiences. If they haven't grabbed me in the first ten pages, the rest goes unread.'

'So, trust is important to you?' I pushed a little more.

'Umm, I think it's more than trust. It's the connection.'

'Perhaps you'd like *Roman a Clef* style as a writing approach?' I suggested.

'I'm not sure,' she responded. 'What is it?'

'It's where the characters are living people, believable, but the narrative weaves around imagined situations and events. Something like Fitzgerald or Hemingway's writing.'

'I like Fitzgerald more than Hemingway. I don't like Hemingway, the man or much of his work. Wait, I take that back. *The Old Man and the Sea* was a masterpiece, and he was a great writer. I'm judging him far too harshly, and who am I to do that.'

'Having an opinion on a writer is not the issue,' I said. 'So long as you have your reasons well thought out. But I'm curious, what about Hemingway, don't you like?'

'It comes down to how he treated women. It seemed like they were objects of desire or trophies to be owned and displayed. The misogyny made him a right bore, which doesn't sit well with me.'

'Do you think he would have been as good a writer in another time?'

'Hard to say,' she surmised. 'Maybe he didn't hate women, and he would possibly argue that he was passionate about them and loved them. But I don't think he appreciated or respected them, and they were play-things for him.'

'How so?' I asked.

'Take his descriptions of Brett in *Fiesta*,' she said. 'He focused so much on what she wore and how beautiful she was but missed the deeper person. Maybe that's because he simply couldn't imagine a woman as smart or intelligent as him, an equal. Maybe he is a product of his time.'

'Like you, I agree with his talent,' I said. 'But I can't get past the dialogue, which wasn't believable.'

'Can't disagree,' Kat responded.

'Maybe that's a by-product of his understated writing style.'

'That could be true,' she said. 'But for me, it is difficult to separate the writing from the man. Maybe that's my weakness.'

'I think that's important to think about,' I said. 'Ok, let's agree his journalism background influenced his writing style, and the facts-and-only-the-facts style influenced writers of the time and those that followed?'

'Yeah, I can live with that.'

'Maybe what was also important was who influenced his writing,' I said.

'How so?' Kat said.

'Ezra Pound was hugely influential. He helped Hemingway erase the dull sentimentality from his writing and pared back the layers to create simple imagery, allowing the reader to create the meaning. Maybe that influenced why his dialogue seems jumbled, confusing in parts.'

'I'm not sure why he was listening to Pound. He was a Nazi sympathiser, wasn't he?'

'Hemingway never forgave him for it,' I said. 'But he was able to divorce the writer from the person.'

'I see your point,' Kat relented.

Whatever the annoyance she carried into the room twenty minutes earlier had indeed passed. Replacing the frustration of interruption was a growing sense of admiration. I liked her curiosity and intellect, and I missed these conversations as writing and lecture deadlines shut me away from people.

'I know you're busy, and talking about writing is great,' she said. 'But I don't want to take up any more of your time. That's why I am here, and I need your help with a thing I'm struggling with.'

'Argh, yes, the thing,' I said.

'Sorry, a little vague, I know. We have an in-class writing task for next week's literature tutorial; the last one didn't go well. I didn't think it was bad, but it didn't impress my writing instructor.'

There was no need to ask who the instructor was. If I had, it wouldn't have come across the right way. This was not about taking sides, so I took a different tact.

'How did it make you feel when she told you what you didn't do well?'

'Like I wasn't good enough to be here, to be a writer,' she responded.

'Why are the words we write for ourselves so much better than those we write for others?' I mumbled as I stepped from my chair, grabbed my coffee and laptop sitting atop unmarked assignments and headed for the inner sanctum of the lab. 'You have your laptop with you, right?' I asked, passing through the doorway without looking back.

'Yes,' she replied, unzipping her backpack and removing the laptop before joining him in the empty lab.

'Ok then, let's see what you can do.'

'Sit!' I said, opening my laptop.

The ageing hinge begged for sympathy each time, resisting and squeaking its tangible displeasure. My aging mediator had served me well, but its time was nearly up, and perhaps it would have even welcomed its inevitable demise. But buying one here was far too expensive. That would have to wait for a trip home.

As the start-up screen slowly wound through its process, I wondered if the task, the teacher, or something else bothered her. But the mechanics of her writing didn't seem to be the issue. I'd checked her blog posts: expressive, organised, and eloquent. Maybe it was the pressure. We'd get to that.

I took a sip of coffee. But it had long since lost its essence and most of its spirit. Hot or cold, it was caffeine. After all, people ordered cold coffees like they were gunpowder milkshakes. But any semblance of protest had long been subdued to appease the addiction. I sensed Kat's growing nervousness as she sat, fidgeting uncomfortably across the table. But that's what I wanted: to place her in a similar situation to the classroom. They say every writer experiences some form of writer's block, much like putting yips. Your brain simply misfires or can't fire at all. There was no blue pill for that. But I didn't have much experience with writing impotence. There was the one time I struggled over a paragraph for ten minutes, though that could have been a case of mild indigestion. Maybe it was as simple as getting her to relax into the process. She might realise fear is simply excitement without breath. Getting her to draw in that fear and breathe out creative expression might cajole the words onto the page.

My screen displayed far too many files, haphazardly arranged. It was another thing to add to the to-do list. A click of the Word icon created a new file. A slight shuffle in the chair straightened my back for comfort, and I began punching the keys hard like an old typewriter. I typed furiously. Kat sat back, stunned at the ease of the performance before her.

'Ok, go ahead,' I said with a nod that would somehow unleash words onto the screen.

'Go ahead and do what?' She responded.

'Write!' I said, punching the keys as words flowed onto the page.

'What are you doing?' She asked.

'Writing, like you'll do when you start punching those keys.'

She sat upright, eyes glaring at her tormentor.

'Is there a problem?'

'No, I'm just thinking,' she said.

'Oh, there's no thinking. That comes later.'

I continued in earnest, pages filling at a clip.

'Writing's not about thinking,' I continued. 'You write the first draft with your heart, get your ideas down on the page. Then, you rewrite with your head. So, the first rule of writing is to write, not think.'

I stopped typing and read through the text on the screen, noting some parts to improve, then spun the computer around to Kat. She sat stunned, slowly scrolling down each page.

'Oh my God, how?' Kat said.

'Do me a favour and print that out,' I said, satisfied with the first part of the lesson.

I walked to the printer in the room's back corner, waiting for each page to wind slowly onto the tray. But being hyped up on writing made me impatient. An old machine was doing what old machines do, just far too slowly for my liking. I turned my attention to the coffee maker idling beside the office door and topped up the remaining contents. I grabbed the pages, gave them to Kat, and continued to the office. I watched through the glass as she read the contents. She stared at the screen, and the cursor blinked its displeasure. Inspiration was as far into the distance as it had ever been. I fumbled around in the office, rearranging books, sorting papers, and adding some to the filing cabinet. Hovering at the door, I sipped the warm contents of my cup slowly. That brief pause turned into pacing around the room's perimeter, pretending to inspect the computers lining the walls.

'Is it possible you could sit down,' she said. 'You're making me even more nervous.'

'Much like you'd experience in a writing test?'

'Yes, and I don't like it … Ok, I get it.'

Kat sighed, and her eyes returned to the blinking cursor and blank page. A few minutes became twenty. She typed a few words, then deleted them. The start remained elusive. I returned to the office and opened the filing cabinet again. There would be no deposit this time. The old-grey cabinet squealed. Looking through the fishbowl, it seemed like the cabinet had devoured me with my head and shoulders deep in its cavernous jaws. I removed a fistful of papers from the rear of the middle drawer and sorted them. Only five needed stapling as I returned to the lab and placed the papers next to Kat.

'*Six Degrees*,' she said, reading the title. 'What is this?'

'Start typing the first couple of sentences,' I responded. 'Sometimes typing a few words can release you from thinking about what to write. It'll get you from one sentence to the next. When you have your own words, start typing. Before you know it, you'll have a paragraph, then a page. Trust me, that horrible little voice you keep hearing will be silenced, and you'll be on your way.'

Kat tapped the keys, slowly at first, then quicker, matching my steps back to the office.

'Punch those bloody keys!' I yelled, passing through the doorway.

The sound echoed throughout the empty lab. She looked up, startled. Across the room, Kat saw only a pair of shoes poking above the windowsill as I settled into the comfort of my leather chair. Inside, I closed my eyes, hands waving as though conducting an orchestra. But there was no music flowing from the lab, only melodic taping and, hopefully, the prose coming to life.

'Yes, yes. That's what I want to hear. Writing!'

Kat's eyes remained fixed on the screen as though any pause would stop the watershed of ideas. The thinking was now far in her rear-view mirror. One page turned into two. An hour passed, and then no sound of typing came from the lab. Only the whirring of the printer had replaced the silence as one page after another flowed onto the tray. There were five pages in total. She arranged them neatly, folding the righthand top edge to bind them. She took a deep breath and knocked on the door. I looked up from editing a manuscript and smiled.

'How did that feel?'

'Good,' she responded. 'I could almost see the scene unfolding before my eyes.'

We both smiled, comforted by the fistful of pages. I reached for a red ballpoint pen and went to work. Each word, sentence and paragraph were carefully considered. It wasn't just about reading the work but respecting the author. Kat said nothing, sitting quietly and watching as I circled the room. I negotiated the labyrinth of my life's work. When one obstacle halted my path, I simply sashayed in a new direction until the next mountain shunted me in another. I paused at two stacked boxes. Each one was labelled in blue letters 'International Courier'. The boxes helped support me momentarily as I marked the paper and continued to meander.

'That took way longer than I thought,' Kat said. 'Felt like I've already done six degrees.'

I didn't answer or even acknowledge what she said.

'Oh, you're in that place where you can't hear me. I could ask you anything right now, like why you moved here, why you're not married, why we never see you out other than getting a coffee or in the classroom. I could even ask you why you criticise academics and universities so much, yet you're one of them?'

'You've started several sentences with the conjunction *but*,' I said, interrupting her list of queries. 'You shouldn't start a sentence with a conjunction.'

'Sure, you can,' she responded.

'No, it's a firm rule.'

'No, no, no! It *was* a firm rule, and now it's more of a convention, so it can be ignored if the writer chooses. You can use a basic conjunction at the start of a sentence for effect, and it can make that sentence stand out for the reader. *And* that is maybe what I intended to do.'

'But you've got to be careful. What's the risk?'

'Well, the risk is that it can be overused,' she responded. 'It may become a distraction, confuse the reader.'

'How?'

'It could create a run-on feeling for the reader when that's not my intention. The rule for conjunctions, *like, and*, or *but*, at the start of sentences is up to the writer. *And* what they were trying to do with it.'

I circled, slowed and stopped next to her. I handed her the papers and sat down in my chair. She read the comments, momentarily pausing at the bottom of the last page. Two words held her attention.

'Well, done!'

Kat smiled and nodded in agreement, and took a deep breath. A weight lifted from her heavy heart.

'You've done something quite remarkable,' I said. 'You've taken something I created and made it your own. That's quite an achievement.'

'Thank you.'

'The first sentence and a half are mine, right?'

'Yes.'

'And it wasn't so much that academics changed,' I said, confirming I'd heard the questions. 'They've always been selfish. It's a competitive world that attracts and magnifies the worst of these people's narcissistic tendencies. If you're not competing for funding, you're competing for attention. It's universities that changed. Profits over standards. Turning learning and ethics into the muddled waters of business and immorality.'

'Universities have to survive, don't they? So, they need to make money.'

'Yes, but it shouldn't be at the expense of standards.'

'Do you think students get what they pay for?' Kat asked.

'If all they're here for is a piece of paper, then I guess so. But it's more than that, and it must be more than that. It means more to you, right?'

'What do you mean?'

'You're not the first-in-family degree holder, but others will be, and that means more to you than just a degree.'

'How do you know I am not?'

'It's a lot of things,' I responded. 'The way you act, the way you think, the way you express yourself.'

'My father and his brother are lawyers.'

'That confirms what I'm saying. Opportunity means success, and you'll make the most of the opportunity. More so than most would. A better job and more money mean a better life for families.'

'That's true! But there's got to be a balance.'

'Yes, but we've lost some foundations, which feeds into academic insecurities and arrogance. Universities tell academics to find research dollars, consult, and publish. That's part of what we do, but not at the expense of our basic values. After all, a university is about learning and students. Without those foundations, it's just buildings full of egos.'

'All admirable comments, but they don't fit the model. Nor do you, I would venture.'

'No, I never did.'

'Well, you ain't gonna see anything different here.'

'Ain't gonna,' I protested. 'What sort of language is that? You were doing so well up until now.'

'I was just messing with you, a joke,' she said with a disarming smile.

'Ok, good. Let me know how you go with your writing test.'

Kat re-read the final red marks on the paper. As they say, an expression is worth a thousand words. Perhaps, in this case, just two.

'Is there anything else,' I said.

'Yes, but not about my writing. It's about yours.'

'Ok, what's on your mind?'

'How'd you get to this?' She said, still clutching desperately to the 80gsm lifeline that harboured the mystery that had breathed life into her writing existence.

'You're asking something you should never ask of a writer.'

'What's that?'

'You've rephrased it delicately, but that doesn't change the essence of "where you get your ideas from". That's what you were asking, right?'

'Yes, that's what I am asking. Why shouldn't I ask that question of you or any writer?'

'Writers are awful to people to answer that question,' I said. 'Why? Because we do that in a writerly way. We get mean, make fun of you, or include you as a character in our novels. Either way, it won't be a pleasant experience for you.'

'I'm not afraid,' she responded.

'You should be, and that is the point I'm making. We don't like that question because we don't know, which embarrasses us.'

'Why?'

'Because we are scared the ideas will disappear into the ether from which they came. Every author responds differently if you can get them to talk about it. Some say they get their ideas from the Ideas Shop on 4th and Bleeker; others say they get theirs from an Ideas of the Month subscription. Every month, an idea arrives in the mail.'

'Rather flippant, but I see what you mean.'

'In truth, I think ideas turn up at the most unexpected times, usually while you're doing something else,' I said. 'There's a fascinating guy who has now passed away, unfortunately. An NYU professor, di Luzio, whose work on demystifying creativity is fascinating.'

'Anyone who can shed some light on that is worth listening to,' Kat responded.

'Let's see if I can remember what he said. It's all about the eureka moment. That flash of an idea comes just before bed or when we wake in the middle of the night. These flashes are significant, but most ignore them as irrelevant, static, and retrievable. They're not! When they come, we need to write them down immediately. You must listen to your subconscious; it works when you're not. It's not that we don't believe in ourselves or the validity of these little ideas, kernels of inspiration. But write them down so you get to the first stage of the creative process, the "what if" question.

'The what if?' She asked.

'Yes, what if a werewolf bit your main character, Jane?'

'Ok.'

'Then she bit into a sandwich. Would the egg and lettuce concoction become a wearwich? What if it came to life at night and started prowling the streets looking for a victim? How would you explain the dismembered body of a vagrant and the blood trail leading to a lifeless sandwich a few metres away?'

'Far-fetched.'

'Yes, but don't dismiss the idea or its potential. But that's another conversation for later. Speaking of sandwiches, it's time for lunch.'

Several students entered the lab and smiled as I exited the room and into the covered pathway. A glance to the left saw Kat heading toward the small convenience store and the car park. Veering right, I walked towards the teaching buildings, then peeled off to the library and the canteen. Most days, the afternoon would be partitioned by a walk home, lunch, and a short nap. That had become a workable habit of getting two days in one. But today, that opportunity had passed with the time taken in the lab. So, grab some food and return to work.

It wasn't fancy or nutritious, but it was filling and fresh. The canteen was housed under a sizeable umbrella structure and full of students no matter the time of day. Most of the seating had been taken, but several places remained in the back rows of three-abreast, picnic-like wooden tables. The location wasn't perfect, but the timing was good. One thing you can take for granted is the fast turnover of students and food; eat and run to the next class.

'Out of noodles, it looks like,' I said to the server. 'I'm a bit late, I guess.'

'A few minutes and there'll be a fresh batch for you,' said the woman, sweating the kitchen that backed onto the serving area.

'No problem! I'll wait back over there until it comes out.'

'Don't go too far. It won't be long,' the woman responded. 'I'll do up a plate; you can pick it up at the cashier.'

A plate of steaming beef noodles sauntered from the kitchen and was handed to the cashier, who gestured to me. A small table in front of the cashier offered flimsy steel spoons and forks and a selection of condiments—chilli oil, jalapeños, soy sauce, ketchup, and sugar. Each would add a bit more zest and flavour to the plain-tasting food. At worst, it would introduce some texture and visual appeal to the beef slivers hidden under the snaking pile of noodles. To be honest, the only way to be sure that spices improved the flavour was not to add them, which only required a one-time misadventure. But sometimes, not even a liberal helped boost the flavour. Eating at the canteen was a trade-off of convenience, quality, and cost. The other option was the coffee shop, which would have taken longer. But it didn't matter today as I dropped the cleaned plate on the unwashed pile at the service area entrance. A glance to the heavens checked for rain. Clouds had gathered and looked dark and heavy, but no rain yet. My pace slowed to a stroll but outpaced students ambling to class. Some slight of foot helped me weave my way around the small clusters of people and to the school's office.

CHAPTER 10

A stack of photocopies sat on the front desk as flashes of light slithered under the copier lid, but that couldn't be all.

'How long will it take for the photocopies to be ready?' I asked the administration assistant.

'Sorry, a few minutes, maybe five, and they'll be done,' she replied from inside the outer office. 'Printing the final run now.'

'Ok, I'll check my pigeonhole and be outside when they're done.'

New staff are allocated whichever pigeonhole was not in use. My spot was on the top right-hand side, above my eye-line, and challenging to reach. It's inconvenient, but time will change that. It was easy to miss a single sheet of paper, especially something important from the university. I reached into the back of the space and pulled a brown-speckled envelope to the front with my fingertips. It was sealed with a handwritten, misspelt name scrawled on the front of the envelope. There were no other markings. It wasn't official, so I tucked it under the pile of photocopies for later.

The administrative assistant exited the room and placed the remainder of the still-warm photocopies on the others. The delay cut into preparation time, so the stopover at the office would be quick, with enough time to grab lecture notes and USB.

By mid-afternoon, the class was done. I found the letter, flipping it over to see if there was a sender's name and address on the reverse side, but there was none. The letter opener slid easily along the top. Inside was a one-page typed note, and curiosity had been replaced with something else as I read the letter.

Doctor,

We know all about what you have been up to with a married woman. We are not going to stand by and watch this happen. It's not right that you are sleeping with a married woman. We'll report you to the university president if you don't stop. You'll be deported. The university knows about you. You are not right to be here. We don't want to see you teaching our kids who has no morals. You have two weeks to resign and leave Fiji.

Signed: Concerned citizens

A threat, it was most certainly. Serious, perhaps, and it didn't take more than a second to find Letitia's number. It rang twice.

'Hey! How are you?' she answered. 'Everything ok?'

'Sort of, but something's come up. We need to chat.'

'You sound worried. What is it?'

'I found a letter in my pigeonhole today with a threat to fire me.'

'Seriously,' Letitia responded. 'Why? Can you read it to me?'

'Give me a second, and I'll take a photo and send it to you.'

The camera wobbled slightly as the cropping took a moment to organise. The lens zoomed in on the paper and captured the threat. Within a second, it was sitting in Letitia's inbox, and it took only a fraction longer to get a reply.

'Who do you think sent it?' She asked.

'I'm betting it's your husband.'

'Hmmm, I don't think he's smart enough to write something like that.'

'I don't think it takes brains to threaten someone. Quite the opposite, and your husband's desperate to keep you.'

An assurance it wasn't him seemed genuine but unconvincing. Over the weeks, he'd escalated the harassment. A few texts became hundreds a day. It would start with tender words, asking what she was doing. That soon shifted to anger when she didn't respond immediately. Kindness turned to accusations, asking who she was with, demanding her to respond. No consideration was given to how busy she was. He thought she was with me, and he wasn't wrong. He wanted her back. For that reason alone, her dismissal seemed ill-considered. She knew him better than anyone, but perhaps her judgement was clouded. Lingering in the background was a warning: never, ever underestimate someone who is cornered.

'Then who could it be?' I asked.

'I don't know, but I'm certain it's not him.'

'Do you think he might have asked someone at the university to do it for him? It was hand-delivered. Does he know anyone here who would help him write the letter?'

'I don't think so. He's taken no interest in meeting anyone there. He never came to any university events, just turned up in his car to take me home.'

'It's a small place, and everyone knows everyone, including everyone's business,' I said.

'Maybe someone helped him,' she said. 'I don't want you to lose your job.'

'I don't think we've done anything for that to happen, but I think the threat is real and could cause problems for both of us. I need some advice just to be certain.'

'Who do you trust?'

'Only one person.'

'Davis!'

'Yes, ma'am.'

CHAPTER 11

There are few certainties in life, even less so when considering those you meet in the corridors of a university. Sometimes, you connect at a level where you bond instantly. It's rare, but it does happen. Davis was one of those people, an American with a personality that matched his two-metre frame. Generally, two alpha males would be unworkable. But alpha-ness comes in different forms. Sometimes, it's mutual respect or maybe something else.

We'd met in less than favourable circumstances. Events draw professors and staff for many reasons. Some attend because it's interesting, others informative or for networking. That day, the event was well attended. It takes time to corral everyone into a room and settle them for the presentation. So, starting times become flexible quickly. If the event starts at 9am, it's a suggestion of possibility, not of certainty.

Arriving at the Holiday Inn conference room twenty minutes late was a safe bet. Some thirty or forty people mingled around the entrance, talking in small groups or pairs. Others took part in the free food laid out on the tables. Fresh fruit, coffee and pastries filled the tables at the entrance to the room.

A quick look inside the conference room confirmed the party was outside, with only the three presenters and a few hotel staff gathered around the stage. I sat on the couch at the hotel entrance. More people arrived, and the noise grew louder, with animated conversations springing up from all corners of the foyer. The lack of urgency became too much for one of the invited speakers, who asked the organiser to announce the conference would begin in five minutes. The Master of Ceremonies tried to explain the situation to the main presenter but insisted that an announcement be made.

'Ok,' a voice boomed over the microphone. 'We are running very late, so please take your seats, and we can get started. We have a lot to do today.'

It was polite, but the voice was touched by frustration. Most simply ignored the request and continued with their conversations and eating. For many, the day was about relationships, not attendance. I thought that grabbing a sandwich and a coffee for morning tea would suffice, and I headed for a vacant chair at the back left-hand corner of the conference room.

The speakers mingled nervously on one side of the stage. One gestured to the MC to start the introduction by pointing at his watch and then rolling his hands to get things moving. The MC reached the microphone and began introducing the speakers and topics for the morning session. Unlike others, I settled into my seat, eating the sandwich and sipping the coffee. I wasn't interested in socialising, just a break from my enforced hermit existence. Besides, a complimentary breakfast always enticed me; it was worth the twenty-minute ride to the hotel.

I looked up from what was left of the sandwich and checked the room. My position allowed me to survey everything and everyone. The seat had other advantages, with it well placed for a quick exit.

'Finally, we can get underway,' the lead speaker said. 'We have a busy schedule today, so let's be mindful of sticking to our schedule. I know it's difficult for you, but let's pretend we are working to that.'

It could have been easily dismissed as lacking local knowledge, but I registered arrogance, which didn't surprise me. International speakers rolled through the university regularly. Some were excellent, others good, but some were indifferent or rude. But being annoyed is one thing; insensitivity and superiority another. Each speaker finished their presentation. If they'd taken some notice, they might have felt the tension in the room. Maybe it was just about presenting the content. Then came the question-and-answer session. That's when things got interesting.

'I'm sure you have lots of questions, given technology is quite new to you all,' the lead speaker said, returning to the microphone.

Everyone in the room squirmed in unison. Murmurs rolled throughout the audience. I eavesdropped on the trio sitting in front of me. They were not talking about the content but the speakers. A few minutes passed, and no questions. I fidgeted in my chair; I wanted to ask a question but didn't want to attract attention.

'Perhaps everyone is still a bit drowsy this morning,' the lead speaker said, again misreading the room. 'Would anyone like to say something, anything? A comment or question, perhaps?'

At that point, most people had had enough. A few left their seats and exited the room. I raised my hand and waited for a response, but it didn't immediately attract the speakers' attention. Perhaps their view was obscured, but that wasn't true. I stood up. Now they couldn't ignore me. But still no acknowledgement.

'You're right,' I said loud enough to be heard from the back of the room. 'Like most, I am feeling a little tired this morning. It was an early start, but no lack of interest or sleep. You make several good points. We can all agree that technology can enhance education, but you may have misunderstood the context here.'

The lead speaker took a step forward with a look of surprise and even more annoyance. He stepped sideways to size me up, and his response seemed one of disappointment rather than interest. I didn't care much for his answer, but it did heighten his resolve.

'Perhaps I should come a little closer so you can see me,' I said as he stepped into the isle and walked a few paces toward the stage.

No one was backing down. Confrontation is always a matter of context. All you need is the right trigger; the first to speak would lose the strategic high ground.

'I'm sorry; maybe you misunderstood my intentions,' the speaker offered a half-hearted apology.

'I think it is pretty clear to everyone what you meant,' I responded.

No one moved in the room, and the murmurs stopped. Whatever happened next would define where this skirmish would go. De-escalation was the better option. I asked myself if this was a hill worth dying on. It seemed now a certainty.

'What's not clear to me and us, I feel, is how we as educators can use technology to enhance learning in our specific context,' I postured. 'To me, and maybe I've misread your focus, it appears your presentation tells us how to use technology in *your* learning context. I understood that today's seminar would also focus on adapting the technology for our context and purpose. I'm sorry, but I don't see how you achieved that in your presentation. Perhaps it would be beneficial to us if you responded to that aspect. What do you think?'

I stepped back and sat down. A slight movement at the end of the row caught my attention. I glanced down the aisle, and a dark figure rocked back on his chair. The man's look was non-committal at first, then a smile beamed across the expanse. A nod offered support, and a raised cup confirmed it. At least one person in the room wasn't pissed at me.

The focus remained on the speakers as each one responded to the question. A hunched figure made his way down the aisle.

'I'm Davis,' the man said, extending his hand to me. 'Can I sit?'

'Sure,' I said.

'Nice work, brother. I thought today would be just a bunch of boring presentations, and then you made it much more interesting.'

'Maybe I was out of line,' I responded.

'Not all,' Davis said.

'I wasn't going to sit back and see another self-absorbed arsehole make a dumb assumption about the audience. We deserved better.'

'You were spot on,' Davis said. 'That's what he did, whether he meant it or not. I think he's probably regretting that approach right now. Besides, I think people here are usually too polite, and it needs to be done. You're officially my new hero, my friend.'

'I'm no hero, just a big-mouth foreigner. But stupidity annoys me.'

'I can tell,' Davis said. 'You'll be pretty busy managing and curbing your annoyances here. This shitshow is on them, not you, and that's why you're the man.'

'I may now be an enemy in my home country after this. That's on me.'

'Speaking of which, I think it's time to move on. Let's grab a drink and avoid any collateral damage.'

It was a moment that bonded the two of us as brothers. And when I needed advice, I turned to the source.

CHAPTER 12

'Let's go for dinner tonight,' Davis texted. 'My buy.'

'Ok, let's make it a place with a bar. I need a drink.'

'Oh, that kind of dinner," he said.

'I need some advice, and I trust you can give me some direction.'

Both taxis pulled up head-to-head outside the entrance to the Indian Curry House and Bar. It was the best choice for food and easy to find. It also had the advantage of being far enough along Victoria Parade to avoid the drunkenness and foreplay that always started earlier on a Friday night. Neither of us had eaten there before, but Letitia's recommendation ensured the food would be good. Any Indian restaurants that littered the inner-city area, of which there were many, offered authentic fare from all parts of the continent. But the one with the least foreigners always provided something better.

We greeted each other the only way we'd known, grasping hands with Davis pulling me into his vast frame, almost smothering me. Watching from afar, a towering black man blanketing the smaller of the two might have thought it quite strange. Not everyone is comfortable with that kind of physical contact, but that's how it was, no matter where or who was around.

The restaurant's *special* wafted down from the kitchen to the next floor. It drew customers up the stairs that turned right, four more steps that led to a small landing and the entrance. A young girl wearing a dark brown T-shirt with the restaurant's logo emblazoned in yellow greeted us with a welcoming smile.

'Are you here for food or drink?'

'Both,' I responded.

'Do you have a reservation?'

'No, do we need one?' Davis joined in.

'No, but we don't have a table just yet. Would you mind waiting at the bar?'

'That'll be fine. No rush,' I responded.

From the bar, the intoxication wafted throughout the restaurant. Frying the sulphur-like compounds within spices of curry and cumin released the aromas into the air, simultaneously suffocating and reviving anyone within breathing distance of the kitchen.

I scanned the top shelf. No high-end whiskies were found. If there's one truism full of certainty, there's no such thing as a bad whisky. There're only whiskies that aren't as good as others.

The double shot splashed lightly into the bulbous tumbler, making for an agreeable interlude from the calamity surrounding us. The light scent fought hard to counter its bolder big brother. I nosed the glass and inhaled the sweet, smoky flavours of the light amber. There's nothing like its bold flavour and intense burn to remind you that you're alive. I savoured its perfection.

We sipped and spoke loudly over the clanging of pots and pans from the kitchen, conversations coming from the small corridor to the right and the large, crowded room behind us. A waitress interrupted a second round and pointed to a small table at the rear corner of the larger room. As they walked through the jigsaw of tables, conversations slowed, and eyes followed. Davis smiled and nodded to no one in particular.

'So, what's the urgency?' Davis said, ignoring the attention.

'I need some guidance.'

'Sounds serious.'

'It might be, I'm not sure.'

I wound through what had happened, focusing on the letters as I handed them across the table to Davis, who scanned it, a skill any worthy academic had mastered. He folded the letter and placed it on one side of the table. His hand rested on the contents as a counterweight to what lay within. He said nothing, instead taking another sip of the second round of drinks.

'What do you think?' I asked.

'Let's backtrack a little. I need more detail. Now tell me everything. Don't leave anything out. Nothing! Do you understand? I need to know it all, or I can't help you. I've been in this situation before, so let's see how deep the rabbit hole goes.'

The tone was no longer playful. Davis picked up the letters and searched for more subtle details in the threats. My eyes wandered around the room, taking in anything that would calm him. But the timing couldn't have been worse, even if I'd done nothing wrong. The whispers of sex-for-grades had grown louder over the past month. Ask around, and people have heard the rumours. Davis had confirmed them. But no one seemed to know anything definitive or were unwilling to put themselves in the spotlight. But when the whispers grew louder, people started to listen.

'Remember that night we all met at Onyx,' Davis said.

'Yeah, it was a great night.'

'What I remember is how Letitia looked at you. I can't remember anyone ever looking at me like that. With every word and every gesture you made, she listened and watched. And you, my friend, you were consumed by her. I've seen you with other women, but the way you two moved in synchronicity, I'd never seen that before. You love her, don't you? Am I wrong?'

Davis was closer to the truth than he could have imagined. People spend their lives searching for something special, someone they want to spend the rest of their lives getting to know. It felt good, right, perfect.

'Yeah, she's the one,' I confirmed. 'She means everything to me, and you're right. She's who I want to be with, but there's that little issue of being married.'

'Yeah, a slight bump in the road,' Davis responded. 'Have you discussed what the future holds for you and her?'

'Yeah, we have, but it's complicated, to say the least.'

'No shit, bro. Look, I'm pretty sure you're ok with the university. You've done nothing wrong from what you have told me. But you need someone on your side if things go sideways.'

'I can sense a very large *but* coming.'

'If these people want you gone, they'll do whatever it takes to get rid of you,' Davis said. 'No matter how innocent or righteous you think you are, they'll burn you in any way possible. It won't matter what's true and right anymore; it'll come down to who will take the fall. That, my friend, is you if you don't plan for what's coming.'

Forging a career as an academic requires good research, skilful teaching, and generous mentoring. Much like politicians, they set out to do good. That approach works for some, though far too few—but there is a much easier way. Universities sing the praises of meritocracy, but they all dance to a very different tune. The reality is that they do everything to reward and protect the most destructive, abusive, and uncooperative people. These scholars poison the well of departments, programs, and individual lives. The more they act up, the more universities double down on their predatory behaviour to please and appease their narcissistic whims. Universities are willing to compromise their values and reputations and alienate their alums to protect bullies and abusers. Wrongly, they think reputation management demands that such behaviour be hidden away from prying eyes. Still, they should know that the scandals will break eventually and that a cover-up would make them look worse. That doesn't deter them from hiring people with full knowledge of abuse allegations against them. That investment in keeping secrets puts their students and staff in harm's way.

It's so easy to be seduced by this upward toxicity as you watch other less talented and more connected climb the ladder of success. If you are the sort of person who likes harassing less powerful people, you'll enjoy it. It is not necessary to be a genius scholar or administrator. When enough people buy into the elaborate fiction of irreplaceability, everyone plays along to get along and hopefully avoid unwanted attention from those feeling threatened by colleagues and students who are more brilliant, productive, or collegial. These people, in turn, internalise the message that they are inferior and will be too busy dealing with their shattered confidence to pose a threat.

Further indiscretions—even crimes—will be kept quiet through regimes of fear and threats of lawsuits, repercussions, and closed-off career opportunities. People cave to the fear, and why not, as they become implicated in shared guilt and work to maintain silence whether they want to. Colleagues who used to get along fine resent their mutual failure to stand up to the bullies. Upward toxicity can work in any profession, but it is particularly effective in a career with few escape routes. If students and colleagues want to avoid these workplace monsters, it means moving families to another country or abandoning their lifework altogether. Most are forced to manage this toxicity for the long term.

'First, you need to speak to your Head of School and tell him what you told me,' Davis continued. 'That needs to be done immediately, and don't leave out details, anything, ok, nothing. Put it on record. You can then say you informed your supervisor and sought counsel, which you followed.'

'What do you think he'll say?'

'He knows his business, and he needs you onboard to fulfil his plans,' Davis said. 'He will tell you straight what issues you face. Informing him of your relationship with Letitia shows your professionalism and concern for the faculty and him. Plus, if shit goes sideways, he won't be blindsided.'

A last mouthful of a third double shot emptied the tumbler and numbed some of the worries that bubbled back up with each sip. Davis paid the bill, and we grabbed a taxi back home to Fletcher Road. The taxi paused at the bus stop that marked our divided paths, and I exited toward my apartment. By the time I'd arrived, unlocked the gates and discarded the sweat-laden clothes, the whisky had seeped into the blood. Typically, alcohol makes you stupid in the way that fear does. But not tonight; whisky brought resolve to the soul.

It wasn't the right time to talk, but Letitia needed to know what was happening. It affected her as much as me. She answered the call immediately, and the conversation tracked on for an hour before the whisky loosened some of its grip. I was lucid enough to send an email. Maybe not quite fully coherent, but it needed to be sent. It was short and sweet. I booked a meeting with the Head of School. It is better to be vague than irrelevant. Any more detail might have made him defensive. I was mindful that emails were not the place for such discussions, particularly given it was a university account. In this world, a healthy fill of paranoia is a sixth sense that might just save you. Limit the exposure; a voice kept repeating over and over.

CHAPTER 13

I rose before the sun reached the horizon. After years of writing, I had scripted my early morning discipline. Get the words down early and enjoy the rest of the day. But here, the environment rules over production. I checked my inbox. The response email was just as focused, confirming a 9.30am meeting. I noticed it had been copied to the Assistant Head of School. Did he sense the importance of the issue? The clock ticked past 7am, so there was time to contemplate the possible directions the meeting might take.

I set out on the walk to campus. There was no point rushing, but I was surprised when I arrived early to see the office door slightly ajar. I knocked lightly.

'Come in and grab a seat,' the Head of School said, pointing to two less comfortable chairs in front of his desk.

I sat down and waited for the typing to stop. An occasional pause and shifting of piles of papers interrupted the flow of words on the screen.

'Maybe I should come back when you have more time.'

'No, no, it'll take just a minute. I need to finish this application. It's a visiting scholar in New York and must go today. That's another thing I want to talk with you about, taking over this position while I'm away and maybe permanently.'

'I'm sure it's well deserved and will be approved,' I responded.

'It has to go to the university first, but it shouldn't be a problem so long as you're on board.'

I knew it was always best to say little and complement much. You never quite knew how he would respond to something said, even if innocently stated. But something bothered me. Was it an invitation or an application? Could it be both? Not likely. I'd heard this story before, but this was slightly different. These inconsistencies marked self-promoters' stories, especially when they held together with a litany of vagaries. The more you listened, the more the inconsistencies in the story bubbled to the surface. Details seemed too fanciful at best. But it wasn't worth challenging the constant self-promoting nonsense. Just allow the self-hero worship to wash over and flow on. But it is also not wise to simply ignore it either. It was part of the rounds of silly games academics liked to play. In years gone by, I would have been less amicable to the rule changes and goalpost shifting for the convenience of others. I'd accepted long ago that it was all just an illusion. That realisation was an evolutionary step in consciousness transcending false logic, where everything is deception and possible no matter the dubious morality.

'How long is the posting if you get it?'

'*When* I get it, it'll be for six months, but I might stay longer,' Ravi said. 'That's something we also need to discuss later when this is done, and the university signs off on the sabbatical.'

Ravi went back to typing. I wasn't bothered by his lack of focus on the meeting, given his assistant hadn't arrived. So, I kept quiet. Let him get it done and then focus on the matter at hand. The longer the typing went, the more interesting the bookshelves behind him became. Most books related to poetry, which I didn't recognise or care much about. It had never been my thing. It seemed too clever or just too pretentious to pique my interest. Let those who can do it. Other books did interest me. Maybe I could borrow one or two from the collection. Not surprisingly, the university library struggled to hold any of the latest autobiographies and memoirs and limited creative writing texts. But that only held my interest for a short time as I became again distracted by the chaotic piles of papers on the desk. It resembled my own office, and that was annoying enough. But to his amazement, Ravi seemed to know precisely where each paper was in a pile. He'd simply flick through the documents and pull out the one he needed. He thrust a stapled manuscript in my direction.

'This one is to be published in a leading British poetry journal,' he said, ensuring I recognised his importance. 'It's my third journal publication this year. Have a read, see what you think.'

'Poetry is not my area, so I don't think my views will be useful to you.'

'You're a writer, an academic,' he responded sharply. 'So, what do you think?'

A knock at the door saved me from what seemed a high-risk situation. The Administrative Assistant opened the door and poked her head inside.

'Sonja will be here in a minute or two,' she said. 'Held up in a student meeting.'

No sooner had the door started to close when Sonja slid past the administrator. She didn't need much room. I'd only had a few interactions with her at a meeting or two and occasional social gatherings. But the briefness only heightened expectations. She was organised and to the point. She knew when not to push on issues and when more thought was needed — skills that would serve her well. She'd graduated from a top British school and taken the bait from the Head of the School. For all his shortcomings, Ravi could sniff out talent and sell his vision. He'd offered her the Assistant Head of School, something she'd have to wait ten years or more for at home. Here, she would get the experience and then move on to something better. New Zealand seemed the most likely landing spot for her level of talent, but Australia would offer her whatever she wanted. After a couple of years of publishing, she could negotiate a position anywhere.

'Just give me a minute, and I'll be done here,' Ravi responded without shifting his focus from the screen.

It would, of course, take more than a minute. Sonja and I chatted quietly, something about island-hopping adventures and her partner's teaching at another university. None of them were that interesting, but I tried to listen. Ravi pushed the keyboard to one side, placed the documents he was working on back into the disorganised pile, and looked up. He smiled, which was unsettling as that typically indicated he knew more than anyone in the room. But he had some competition today.

'Ok, daylight is burning, and I need to get this off to New York, so let's get this meeting underway,' he said. 'You called the meeting, so you have the floor, Jack.'

'As the Head of School and my supervisor, I need to inform you of a situation that has escalated to a point where I am concerned about the fallout for the faculty and me,' I said, almost word-for-word from my early morning rehearsals.

I looked at Ravi, whose attention was on his assistant. That look confused me. What was I missing? He then turned back to me and gestured to continue.

'Ok, so what is this escalating situation?' Ravi said.

'There are two things. I must inform you that I am in a relationship with another staff member. We've been seeing each other for about six weeks, and I'm concerned it may become a problem given the gossip and changes to the policies on staff relationships.'

'Yes, the university is pushing to tighten the policy,' Ravi said. 'But the policy isn't the issue; enforcing it is, with no one testing the ground. But I believe the proposed changes might create more problems in some schools.'

'What do the changes focus on?' Sonja asked.

'Basically, it will say, if adopted, that no staff members can have a relationship, and if they do, it is immediate dismissal.'

'You're kidding,' I responded. 'How is that enforceable? It's got to be against human rights. Not to mention impossible to comply with. People will be people.'

'Exactly,' Ravi said.

'How will that affect married couples or have a partner hired by the university but not married?' Sonja asked.

'It won't, but this situation will come under the new rules.'

'Will it be retrospective?'

'I believe they'll try and make it so.'

Again, Ravi's attention shifted to Sonja. I glanced at her to gauge her response. They both smiled. It was almost unnoticeable, but I saw it.

'Ok, what am I missing here? I don't understand what's so amusing?'

'No, we are not laughing at you,' Ravi responded. 'What's amusing is that you think you could hide that from us, from anyone.'

'That obvious, huh?'

'You're kidding, right,' said Sonja, joining in. 'You just have to see you two together, and you know.'

'So, when did this become so obvious to you?'

'That night at the bar, you two were getting cosy in the booth,' Ravi said. 'You didn't see us arrive, did you?'

Going to an obscure dive bar seemed like a clever move. Most people they knew drank at Onyx; an up-scale bar close to the main restaurants but far enough from the seedier strip bars where Chinese prostitutes plied their trade to visiting sailors. The drinks were cheap, especially during happy hour, and the pool tables were mainly straight and true. As the night wore on, the bar became rougher. Letitia and I headed upstairs to a private bar that was much quieter, with darker corners and fewer interested patrons.

Though quiet, other dangers lurked in the more tranquil places. A small group of drinkers were holed up in the corner of the bar. Two thick-set island boys watched as the centre of attention played with three scantily dressed girls. Each one was barely drinking age and certainly out of their depth, but that wasn't the issue. At the centre of the circus was what looked like a wannabe rapper. Now, rappers profess it's all about the music, but equally important is the image. You must stand out in a crowded room of gold chain-wearing thugs. That means having the correct name and dressing the part is just as crucial as rhyming the words. Maybe he didn't have a cool name like 2 Chainz or 50 Cent, but the ringleader embraced the look fervently. So, when someone looks at you, you want to ensure the first thought is, 'Who is this guy? They look like somebody!' He sported a half-sleeve of tattoos, gold chains, rings on both hands, slick hair, mandatory NBA oversized Boston Celtics singlet, not to mention a swagger to match his on-point shoes. But it wasn't the look that people feared. It was so out of place and laughable, to be honest. His father made him far more dangerous. If you were a friend, there was none better. But if you pissed the boy off, you'd get an unexpected visit from the police investigating some trumped-up charge.

Hiding in a corner worked for a while, but the drinking and partying eventually turned spectators into participators. So, we returned to the main bar and found an empty booth until the attention they desperately wanted to avoid arrived.

'You knew from the outset?' I said.

'Pretty much,' said Ravi. 'You should know by now that not much escapes me.'

'Ok, that's one for you, but there is something you might not know,' I countered, trying to re-balance the lost advantage. 'These arrived in my pigeonhole over the last week.'

I now hand two letters to the Head of School. He read them, passing the first to Sonja as he locked on to the second letter. He leant back in his leather business chair, crossed his legs, and stroked his beard. Perhaps, he thought the action could summon a plan, a response, a way forward. He breathed deeply.

'This could be a problem,' he said. 'They're not signed, well, not by the writer. Concerned citizens. What the hell does that mean? Who do you think wrote them?'

'I think it's the husband.'

'That limits its impact and our options.'

'Have you shown these to Leti?' Ravi said.

'Yes.'

'What does she think?'

'She's not as concerned as I am. She doesn't think it's her husband.'

'Why? Seems the most likely suspect.'

'Letitia feels he's not smart or brave enough to try something like this.'

'I think you're right, and that raises the stakes. I feel he's been backed into a corner since you arrived back in town, and he's got the most to gain from exposing you to the university.'

'What do you mean exposing,' I responded. 'I don't think I've done anything wrong. Letitia's not with him anymore; they've separated, as far as I understand.'

'Professionally, you've done nothing wrong. Letitia's not your student, and you're not her supervisor. That's important, but morally, that's another issue, especially here. Islanders can forgive a lot of things, but there are some they hold firm on. This one could be one of those.'

'Is that what you think? I'm morally culpable.'

'It doesn't matter what I think,' Ravi responded. 'I'm not judging you. I'm happy for you both. Sonja says Letitia is happier now than she's ever seen her. That's because of you. But people will judge you no matter what you think. It's in their nature, and this is fodder for gossipers. People will talk, the truth will not be considered, and you'll find it impossible to convince people of anything else.'

'What do you think I should do about the letters?'

'Forget the letters. They're not important now.'

'Forget about them, why? Can't we investigate it, find out who's doing this and warn them off through a lawyer? Send the person a cease-and-desist letter. Something?'

'First, we only *think* it is the husband, though it is likely him. It's typed, so it's difficult to trace. And it's not posted, so that's not going to help. Legally, it's a dead end.'

'Ok, then what are my options, if any.'

'Let's take a step back,' Ravi said. 'Do you know what you're getting yourself into here? You're fighting a battle on three critical fronts. One is the phantom correspondent, and the second is the university; they will find out if they don't already know. We have to assume they do.'

'Right,' I said. 'So, trouble.'

'I can handle the university, but you must write a letter. Admit to the relationship. Inform me officially that you and Letitia are together. Don't go into details, like dates, places, or things. Don't try to justify it. You'll look defensive and, therefore, guilty. It doesn't need justifying. Keep it simple, to the point, and brief. The less you say, the more we can avoid misinterpreting the facts. The point is that you have informed me of your relationship with another staff member. That's it, nothing else.'

'Have I done something wrong? I asked. 'I mean, legally, that might threaten my tenure here?'

'No, I don't believe so. Letitia's not a staff member under your direct or indirect supervision. Sonja supervises her. So that's not an issue; that, my friend, is critical for you.'

'That's promising!'

'Promising, yes, but that's not going to be the end of it. As I said, you have pending problems, and I can't emphasise enough how the third one will be your biggest challenge. The university is not who you will have to convince of your innocence.'

'Who do I need to convince and of what?' I said defensively.

'What I can't provide you is what you'll never know as long as you are involved with her.'

'What's that?'

'A scandal-free life. You know what happened to the last foreigner who had your position. You've been patient and stayed out of harm's way until now. Good for you, but that is done now. If this goes forward, people will talk, and we'll have to deal with that. If so, we have legal options, but it won't look good for you, the university, or me.'

'You think it'll get to that?'

'To be honest, yes, I think, knowing who is pushing the agenda on campus, it is possible,' Ravi said. 'You need to be ready for that. It's going to get ugly, and you'll be closely scrutinised. You must make a choice. Go forward or give her up until she sorts out her life. Divorce, I mean, until she's free. All points covered, legally, morally.'

'Do you think it's that easy?'

'Not at all. Anyone can see how you feel about each other, and that's not in question. You only have to be momentarily in each other's orbit to realise that.'

'You know what she's been through,' I said. 'I can't simply walk away from that, from her.'

'Maybe she just wants to make up for what she's lost. Or simply needs a way to get out, and you're it.'

'That's possible, but that's not her, and I think you know that!' I said.

'Yes, I do. But it comes down to how serious you are. So *how* serious are you?'

'I'm committed, and she says she is too, even if it takes a year to work through all the issues.'

'Are you sure? Give her up, and this goes away. She's not from your world. You've got a good look at what that is now—a jealous husband who's not prepared to give her up. You've got a fight on your hands to keep her. It's going to get messy before it gets better. Is she worth it? Are you up for that?'

'I appreciate your candour,' I said calmly. 'So, these are my options. Give Letitia up or fight for her. Giving her up is not an option. I love her.'

'Does she love you?'

'Yes!'

'Is it sexual?'

'Why does that matter?'

'I need to know how deep you are and whether you can back out of the situation if needed. So, I guess that's a firm no on backing away.'

'Yes, it's a firm no. Are we done with this line of questioning?'

'Yes, with the questioning; no, I'm not done yet. If you take the option to fight, you must protect yourself. I can guarantee the university is going to come for you.'

'How do you know that?'

'I know them and know who's going to lead that charge. She thinks she can get you and me at the same time. So, you need to address that immediately.'

'Ok.'

'You need to understand that everyone might not see it as simply two people falling in love in a complicated situation. Write a letter to me after this meeting. Print it, sign it, and give it to Hanna at the front desk. Tell her she must date stamp it and hand it to me by 5pm. Clear?'

'Just the basics; we're in a relationship, that's all?'

'Yes.'

Sonja handed me the letters and stood up. She turned and placed a hand on my shoulder. Was it reassurance or a warning?

'She loves you,' Sonja said. 'She's much tougher now, and she can take it. We are there for you both. Know that, ok?'

I smiled and watched as Sonja veered left and walked down the hallway toward the administrative office. I turned right and headed down the stairs to the writing lab.

The chair cushioned my landing. A new file appeared on the screen, and I wrote the letter. Short and to the point. It's probably the shortest thing I'd ever produce, but maybe the most important. I grabbed a pen from the holder and signed it before heading back up the stairs to the office and, hopefully, some peace of mind.

CHAPTER 14

This world seems confused by the rules of night and day. Or perhaps it ignores them, refusing to cool as the sun fades to yesterday. It's as if Mother Nature had forgotten to halt the war between night and day and deliver its inevitable acquiescence. But as darkness rolled over the island, the ocean breeze began to subdue the day's heat and humidity. The creeping chill had become so common even for a half-awake body. Instinctively, my foot reached out, curled around the loose-weave cotton blanket and pulled its warmth to cover my shoulders. A blanket in the tropics would seem strange for such a balmy climate. Even in winter, there was little to warrant one. But it had become a regular rescuer. As I rolled over, the blanket followed in kind.

I reached out, searching for the warmth of her body. The cold emptiness of the sheets drew me out of my slumber and to attention. It took a few seconds to adjust the eyes to the semi-darkness of the moonlit room. The clock ticked over loudly to 3.00am. Maybe she'd left early and was back home on the other side of the inlet.

While the frequency and the length of her visits increased, it was never going to be enough. Having her there as the last thing seen before sleep and the warmth of her body in the mornings was happiness. The desire for more had become stronger with each visit—wishful thinking, given the situation. Longer stints volunteering at the women's crisis centre and The One Billion Rising women's movement took up most of her spare time. So, it was Friday nights for dinner and drinks, Saturday morning brunch and the occasional mid-week stay-over, like tonight. Any more would have been expecting far too much. So, no pressure. Enjoy the ride and see where it goes.

As the eyes adjusted, I squinted at the shadowy figure partially filling the end panel of the row of windows. I took in the contour of the line that bound and gave form to her naked body against the starkness of the ultra-white louvres. Her left arm hung loosely beside her defiant leg. The right arm reached up to the louvres at head height. Her hands were not resting on the wooden slats but clutching desperately onto the flat surface as though her life depended on it. Her grip was so tight it accentuated the muscles running down her arm. She stood stone cold, silent, frozen by the night's cool air. Her eyes locked in position, surveying the park for movement. Whatever she sought among the shadows and feint light of the shoreline, swings, and toilets wouldn't escape surveillance.

My eyes followed the curves of her body. Each slice of moonlight kissed the skin until it receded into the dark recesses of the room. What was left was a perfect silver-lined silhouette from shoulder to thigh. She'd said her skin was too dark. That wasn't true. She thought her body was unattractive, which wasn't true either. She wanted to lose weight. She shouldn't. She'd worked hard in the gym to shape her body to match her mind. Four days a week with weights, yoga, and boxing paid off. A point that crashed home all too painfully in the ring. A click of the jaw reminded me of that. She'd taken control of her life, now confident and stronger physically, emotionally, and spiritually.

'Come back to bed,' I whispered, not to startle her. 'You'll catch your death of cold.'

Maybe she heard the whisper, maybe not. She didn't flinch. Not a muscle moved. Her focus remained steadfast on what lay in the creeping shadows of the dark park. She glanced casually back at me.

'Go back to sleep,' she said.

Slipping back under the warm blanket would have been all too welcomed. I was unsettled by her reluctance to return. I swung my legs over the edge of the bed in one motion, and my feet hit the floor.

The cold breeze hadn't yet reached there, and the momentary warmth comforted me. But by morning, that would have changed.

Just two steps, and I was at her side. I lightly touched her shoulder with my left hand and moved closer to her body. Placing one arm around her waist, I cupped her breast with my other hand and pulled her close. I felt her heavy breathing as she tensed up with the warm embrace. I moved my wandering hand to her shoulder to reassure her. She trembled slightly from the brush of my breath against her neck. My left hand dropped from her shoulder to her side, finding her hand. Our fingers entwined as my thumb stroked her wrist as I lightly squeezed her hand. She responded kindly and relaxed enough to allow her head to rest against mine.

'How long have you been awake?' I asked.

'Sorry I woke you?'

'It's ok. I was cold and reached out for you, but you weren't there. I thought you might have gone.'

'I couldn't sleep,' she responded.

'Worried about things?'

No response. Telling her everything would be alright would have been the sensible thing to do. But there was no way of fulfilling that promise.

'What's so interesting out there in the park?' I said, trying to distract her.

'He's out there,' her voice trembled. 'I can't see him, but I know he's there. He's always there. Lurking, waiting in the shadows, spying on me.'

No reply from me would make that feeling go away. Saying it was just her imagination wasn't going to help. Deep down inside, I knew she was probably right. It wasn't too difficult to imagine him following her, watching the apartment, waiting for her. He'd done it before, and he'd do it again. There was little doubt about that. I peered through the gaps in the louvres. I searched for the slightest movement in the shadows of the buildings, trees and seats that lined the footpath next to the stone wall. There were many places to hide and watch the building without being seen. The moon struggled to find its way into the darkened crevices of the park. It was challenging to differentiate a person from a post. Most nights, voices rang out, overpowering the sound of the ocean's ebb and flow. But voices remained hidden as the figure she imagined in the darkness. And no matter what assurances were said, none would divert her from scanning the cars parked along the edge of the road, which separated Apted Park from its residents that lined its inner lines.

Getting her back to the bed's warmth and safety might reassure her. I turned and retrieved the crumpled blanket. Finding the edges, I unfurled it in one flowing motion around her shoulders. She grabbed the edges of the blanket and pulled it tight around her. At that moment, she stopped looking out the window, again lowering her head to my comforting shoulder, and her eyes followed. She relaxed and nestled into me. I kissed her neck, and her dark curls tickled. She pulled my hand back to her breast, and her cold, erect nipple pushed into my warm palm.

'Hold me and never let me go,' she pleaded. 'Please tell me you love me and mean it. Never hurt me, never leave me. I must know you'll be there for me, no matter what.'

Tears rolled down her cheek and disappeared into the recess of her past.

'I meant what I said on the beach,' I said softly. 'I'll wait for you no matter how long it takes, no matter what it takes. Even if you decide it's not me you want, or it becomes too difficult, I'm not walking away. Look into my heart. I'm yours, forever.'

'Let's go back to bed,' she said, finally surrendering her watch.

We slid under the warm embrace of the blanket, protecting us from the coolness of the light breeze. She rolled away momentarily, then looked at me. She said nothing. I wanted to tell her I loved her but hesitated. It was as if she was negotiating the past and the future. She searched for the right thing to say in the right way.

'Did you mean that?' she said.

'That I'd be there for you, yes.'

'I've come so far, yet know there's more to go.'

I said nothing. She was right, and there was more to come.

'I don't want to lose what I've fought for. But how can I make a decision that will hurt so many people? I want to help him move forward, not disappoint my parents and bring shame to them, and I don't want to lose you. It's so difficult.'

Now, the look made sense. She'd prised herself away from one man and was not about to surrender so easily to another. I didn't want that either. There were possibilities, consequences, and responsibilities; no matter what she decided, there'd be a heavy price. She could have quickly given up and surrendered to her jealous husband and her family's urgings to make the marriage work. But she hadn't and wasn't about to either. She wanted a better future and one she could shape. I hoped I would be part of that future. But if not, that would be ok, so long as she found peace and purpose beyond simply someone's possession. She had so much more to offer the world, and it would be a better place.

'I'm not going to say I know how you feel because I don't,' I said. 'How could I? And I certainly don't want to put any more pressure on you. You have enough to deal with. I just want you to know that no matter what you decide, to stay or come to me, I'll support your decision.'

'I know you will,' she whispered. 'You did good, Jack.'

I smiled. She rolled away from him but grabbed my arm, pulling me with her. My hand first found her curved thigh. She relaxed, now warm and secure, and wriggled into my arched body, and my hand slid down her thigh to just above her knee. She clasped it lightly and slowly guided it up her leg, around her thigh and placed it on her breast. Her nipple rubbed against my fingers, but I dismissed the urge to take advantage of the situation. There is a time and place for everything. And while it was the place, it wasn't the time. Or was it?

I closed my eyes and tried to surrender to the night, but it didn't come as my thoughts quickly trailed back to the park. I focused on her breathing, now slow and deliberate. I tried to match her rhythm, which might help him find peace and relax. Then she rolled over toward me. Her hand cradled my cheek as she looked into my eyes and leaned forward. I felt her lips, light to the touch.

'Why do you find me interesting?' she asked.

It seemed like a simple question, but it confused me.

'You're kidding, right,' I said, surprised by the curiosity, if not the honesty.

'No, seriously,' she responded. 'You've travelled the world and done so much. And here you are with me, a girl from a small town with one traffic light that was added last year. I can't help but be curious about why you find me interesting. Don't you think?'

I scanned her face. She was so much more than a beautiful woman. There was something about her, an aura of deep compassion and longing in those eyes, something I desperately wanted to soothe. Is there a thing such as a fatal character flaw that runs deeply down the backbone of life? I didn't think such an archetype existed outside the whimsy of literature or movie narratives. But that might just be true. My weakness: pathological altruism, to the point of recklessness. Was it a weakness or a sickness? I worried it was simply history repeating itself. I desperately wanted to defend the weak and protect the vulnerable, attracting calls of self-righteousness. I had thought such a comment had been a compliment. But I quickly learned that some took advantage of such a character trait. Did that matter? Probably not. I was comfortable standing by her, helping her no matter the outcome. I loved her.

'Do you remember that day I met you walking across the car park?' Letitia said.

'Near the small hotdog stand?'

'Yes, you looked tired,' she responded.

'Yeah, a long flight and a busy couple of weeks.'

'We were so happy when they said you were coming back from Saudi Arabia. Everyone was so excited. But then I hadn't seen you for two weeks, and I wasn't sure if you had arrived. You'd become a mystery, a ghost. People talked about you and mentioned fleeting glimpses of you walking across campus. I looked for you, but I wasn't quite sure if I should visit. Then you were there, hotdog and drink in hand. It was just like I'd seen you yesterday. You looked happy to see me.'

'To be honest, it might have been the pure joy of actually being able to look at a woman's face and talk with her without fear of losing something one cherished,' I replied.

She'd slipped her hand down the inside of my leg to find that he was a little more awake than she'd thought.

'Is this the something you didn't want to lose,' she said. 'I've become quite fond of this.'

'Is that my only asset?'

That playfulness marked the difference from the shy girl just twelve months earlier. Each day, she'd sweep by my office around 10am and glance in as she headed across the corridor to her office. It started with a smile, a wave, and a hello. Her office door would squeak its surrender, and that'd be it most days. Those pleasantries meandered along for two months with little change. One day, she came to the door and chatted briefly. The conversation was trivial, seemingly unimportant in content but not context. The next day, the doorstop changed. She hesitated for a moment, then walked in and sat down. She was so focused on mustering the strength to interrupt there was no apology, though it wasn't necessary. Whatever she wanted was far more important than such trivialities. She wasn't sure what she would or could do after completing her degree. A doctorate was possible, maybe in New Zealand, with a good mentor who could guide her. But for now, the first tentative steps of that plan were in place. She handed me a chapter of her thesis I'd asked for, but she'd been reluctant to share.

'What was it like in Saudi Arabia?' Letitia asked, interrupting my thoughts. 'Is it true women are completely covered from head to toe.'

'Yes and no,' I responded. 'Outside, head to toe with women's hair and face completely covered. There were exceptions, with some department stores allowing women to go uncovered and foreign women only had to cover their hair.'

'I can't imagine wearing that in public,' she said.

'It took a lot of getting used to it,' I said. 'You can only see the eyes and not even that sometimes with a mesh shutting out any enquiring looks. To be honest, I understand why.'

That surprised her more than I anticipated, and it needed a slight adjustment to clarify what he meant. It was rare for a single woman to be seen walking in public. Most times, the black shadows moved as one. Strangely enough, the point of men not gazing upon the women created even more curiosity, at least for foreigners. When opportunities arose, the tendency was to seek out something familiar. The eyes became the focus of that gaze. The wonderment of what lay behind the veil of secrecy never ceased. That mystery made observers even more curious.

'That's how it stayed for a long time,' I said. 'Minimal, if any, interactions. Only twice, in fact.'

'Only twice, the whole time you were there,' she repeated. 'Why? What is the issue? Isn't that a way for us to understand who they are and why they do what they do?'

'We were told from the start that contact with a woman or even speaking to them could mean being exiled from her family. They can only interact with men from their immediate or extended family.'

'So, is it a protection thing or possession thing?'

'Both apply, I think,' I said. 'That's what I meant about understanding but not agreeing with why they do what they do. It's strange how different we are, yet so similar. But that all changed at an international photographic exhibition of Bedouin life.'

CHAPTER 15

As a German colleague, Tim, and I strolled down the aisles of photographs, a woman's voice rang out from behind, startling us. Just a few metres away stood a young woman with long black hair pulled into a tight ponytail. It was as though she'd walked out of a clothing catalogue in London. But that's not what grabbed our attention. She was normal in every way, which stunned us. There was no veil, no hiding, just a young woman in a power suit. Dark grey trousers, a white high-collared shirt, and a tailored jacket that fit snuggly around her waist and faltered to the hips. The image was as powerful as any photograph of the Bedouin foot soldier gazing down from above. Large black and white figures dressed in full desert garb with an old-style single-shot rifle slung across the chest with the barrel northward to the sky. Each deeply tanned face with eyes full of life, hardship, and pride. As she approached, the young woman showed no surprise or hesitation as though it was an everyday encounter. It could have been so except for the warning not to engage with Saudi women.

'Welcome to the exhibition,' she said in a perfect British accent. 'My name is Yasmine, and I am your guide today. We are pleased to have you here, and we hope you enjoy our first exhibition.'

I smiled, but Tim retreated a step and then a third. I said nothing as I watched him fade into the recesses of the exhibition as though pulled to a safer locale to watch my demise. I'd typically have heeded the warnings, but not today. Maybe four months without seeing a woman's face drew me toward Yasmine.

'I'm Jack, and that disappearing man over there is Tim,' I said, struggling with the practised impulse to reach out and shake her hand.

Talking to a Saudi woman was one thing. Touching her was another. I glanced across at the two security guards at the entrance to the exhibition. Each of the men eyed me suspiciously, but they made no advances.

'Thank you for welcoming us, though my friend is a little concerned, please excuse him. What an amazing exhibition. Are these Bedouins?'

'Yes, but they are called *Bedawi* or desert dwellers by local people,' she corrected me.

'Are these current photographs of *Bedawi,* or are they older?'

'Some are recent, taken within the past six months for this exhibition. Others were taken some time ago. Those at the entrance were shot in the 1940s and 1950s. The larger ones closer to us are the most recent.'

'There's little difference,' I observed.

Yasmine walked a few steps toward the largest photograph, a close-up of a Bedouin man with a face more like a topographical map etched with deep contours of long days in the extreme desert sun and heat. Each line carved a valley of experiences few could imagine.

'So *Bedawi* people continue to live a traditional life,' I said.

'Yes, these families do, but there are fewer today. Young people prefer a modern life to the desert and want to work in big cities like Riyadh or Jedda.'

Yasmine walked with me down the rows of photographs, occasionally stopping to point out something in the image or answer a question. I asked about their traditional values and how things had changed. As they came to the end of the last row, she paused.

'Which of the photographs did you like the most?' She asked.

I pointed to the first row of photographs. Strolling back through the exhibition, we slowed and stopped at the largest one: a *Bedawi* elder holding the reigns of a camel. It was hard to tell how old he was; maybe in his eighties, or he could have been older. The man looked past us, out into the distance, as though searching for direction. Perhaps he was contemplating a new future or maybe a lost past.

'I like this one very much,' I said.

'What do you see? Yasmine responded.

'I see a man who has lived a life full of adventure. His eyes are one of wonder. I can't imagine what he's seen or done. But what I can see is a kind of sadness. I wonder if he's lost something or someone.'

'Interesting,' she said. 'That man is my grandfather and still lives that life.'

'So, you are a *Bedawi* but don't live this life. Right?'

'No. My father wanted something different and sent me to study in London. To know more about the new world.'

'Can I ask you a question?' I enquired. 'And please, I don't want to offend. I'm just curious.'

Yasmine smiled as though she was expecting the question. Perhaps it was something foreigners would ask if they had this opportunity. That didn't deter me.

'You want to know why I can be here talking with you without wearing an abaya,' she interrupted.

'That transparent?' I responded.

'Your friend retreated so quickly, and staying far away from us was a big hint.'

We turned together and looked toward Tim, who remained cautious, faking an interest in other photographs at the far end of the exhibition. His nervous glances quickly gave away his concern. Yasmine gestured for him to come over, but he politely declined. We laughed, knowing he wasn't about to change his mind.

'Sorry, my friend is a little concerned about interacting with you,' I said.

'It's ok, understandable,' she replied. 'It took many months to get permission to stage the exhibition and even longer to allow me to be an interpreter.'

'I can only imagine,' I added.

'Actually, it is fortuitous for me,' she said. 'They needed someone who knew the culture and spoke English. None of the men wanted to venture out of the desert, so they asked me. But that meant my grandfather had to come to Riyadh, something he dislikes immensely. It is too busy, too hectic, he says.'

'Allowing you to dress as a foreigner and interact with us must have taken considerable persuasive powers,' I said.

'My grandfather can be very persuasive. He felt that if he was in the exhibition, his granddaughter should be the one to talk about his life.'

'Makes sense,' I said.

'He's a very traditional man, but he knew things needed to change. Today, many Saudi Arabian rules do not translate to Bedawi culture. In the desert, much like life, you need to change to endure.'

CHAPTER 16

Knowing you are born for change is most important. Along that journey, everyone comes to face one's demons and angels. But it is more about knowing yourself and your self-worth than knowing who to trust.

I stopped talking, and Letitia remained silent for a moment.

'You think things are difficult, then you realise there are other ways to look at your problems,' she said. 'Maybe my life's not so bad. Yasmine is an inspiration, and she keeps moving forward despite the obstacles. You never know what the future brings.'

Like most situations, it's a matter of perspective. Harassed daily with hundreds of texts, escalating with each screeching beep, is bound to challenge anyone's mental state. Yet, she'd found a way forward. She created opportunities for herself and fought hard to change her situation. That's what drew me to her. Yes, she was beautiful, and yes, she was brilliant, but above all, she was compassionate, caring, and thoughtful.

'You asked why I think you are so interesting,' I said. 'You feel like home to me. A comfortable feeling that makes me strong when I am with you. Perhaps you don't see the strength I see in you yet, but you will.'

'You think I am strong,' she said as disbelieving as anything I had heard her say.

'Yes. Look at how far you have come and what you've overcome. You want a future that other people have issues with. You may not have worked it all out yet, but something tells me you will.'

Letitia smiled, but I knew it was an embarrassment, not a resolution. That was ok. It wasn't important to convince her of anything; I just wanted her to know she was far more important than others thought.

I glanced at the clock as it shifted past 5am. We rolled over, and within seconds, Letitia was asleep. Like I'd done a million times before, I searched for a good memory that helped me relax and find a way home to that peaceful place. I then surrendered to what was left of the night, and that's how it stayed as we slept through to mid-morning.

Not even the sun's heat had managed to wrestle away the pleasant dreams and thoughts of a life with her. But the running water woke me. I pushed the blanket down to the bottom of the bed, where it would stay until needed. I pulled myself up on one elbow, grabbed the side of the bed and swivelled to a sitting position on the edge of the bed. I took a moment to regain my balance, which was always challenging. The cold floor provided a nice reprise from the heat seeping through the open louvres. The door to the bathroom was open, and I could hear the water cascading onto the blue-tiled floor, gurgling its way down the drain. The shower curtain reeled back, and her face appeared through the gap.

'Coming in?' She asked.

It seemed like a question, but it wasn't. Letitia cocked her right leg around the edge of the shower door and slid it up and down, enticing me from the bed. It didn't take much enticement. Beaded water rolled from her hip to her knee and beyond. Peeking out from just behind the door was the shadowed black and grey tattoo of a Koi running from the lower stomach and disappearing behind her inner thigh. The outline created the illusion of launching itself out of the water as though freed from its comfortable home. She looked down to see what had drawn my attention.

'If you take those clothes off, you can join us.'

The clothes fell to the floor, and I entered the shower to find her leaning against the tiled wall, her legs apart, revealing her perfectly pear-shaped form. She turned and faced the wall, and I slid in behind her, grabbing her hips and pulling her under the cool water. I pushed up against her, wrapping my arms around her waist.

'Push harder,' she whispered as her hand slid down to grab my cheek, pulling me deep inside her.

The water cooled, and so did the desire. I exited the shower and grabbed a towel from the neatly folded pile beside the toilet. I dried off as Letitia stayed in the cubicle. I looked into the mirror, and it reminded me I was losing the battle on two fronts; age should not weary thee, but the evidence was contrary. Perhaps removing the stubble would at least create an illusion of youthful desire. I ran my palm down the side of my face, which quickly faded. I circled the mirror with a hand towel, wiping away the light shadow of mist. The other hand lathered a film of shaving cream over the stubble. The double-edged razor moved slowly over my cheek and curved around the jawline.

'You're bleeding,' Letitia said, tilting my head to one side to reveal a trickle of blood descending to my neck. She thumbed the blood away, but it kept flowing as quickly as it disappeared.

'Old razor?' She asked.

'Old face,' I responded.

'But a handsome one,' she said, grabbing my towel and clipping my cheek with a well-directed snap. She dropped the towel in the basket, pulled a fresh one from the pile, and sat on the edge of the bed, close to the nightstand and her phone.

'When I'm done here,' I said, 'I'll organise breakfast. What do you want? Something cooked. Croissant, coffee?'

'Not sure, I'm just going to check my messages first,' she said, grabbing her phone from the bedside table.

I peered around the corner of the bedroom doorway and watched as she sat cross-legged on the edge of the far corner of the bed, closest to the window. She held the phone in one hand while the other flicked her wet hair from side to side to aerate the long curls, so they dried quickly. She had grabbed one of my black T-shirts, which ballooned over her petite frame, hiding most but not all of her pink satin underwear.

It was never the number of texts that mattered.

'What did he say?'

'The usual,' she responded. 'I'm a whore, bitch, cunt, slut. Whatever insults he could think of. He needs to get a thesaurus. They're becoming old.'

'Is that all he wanted, to abuse you.'

'No, he wanted to know if you fucked me last night like he didn't already know.'

'What did you say?'

'I told him you were a better lover than him, and you had a bigger dick.'

'Oh,' I said, trailing off.

Patience wears thin after a while. Attacking his manhood may not be the way to go. But I wasn't the one receiving the hundreds of insults.

'I know, I know,' Letitia said, responding to my look of surprise. 'Perhaps I shouldn't have, but his abuse is never-ending.'

She looked exhausted and desperate as she shrugged her shoulders. I walked past her to the kitchen.

'Nothing to eat for me,' she said. 'Just a coffee and all this nonsense to stop.'

I didn't respond, lightly touching her shoulder as I passed by. I grabbed the kettle, filled it with water, hit the switch at the base, and heard it kick heartedly into its task. Holding the plunger and the coffee tin in one hand, I gestured with the almost empty milk bottle with the other.

'No, just black for me, please.'

She took the cup, sipped it slowly and closed her eyes as though inhaling its contents would somehow rejuvenate her. After a few more sips, she placed the cup on the breakfast bar and climbed on the smooth surface. The black T-shirt pulled up as she leaned back, exposing her thighs. She said something, but I was far too distracted to hear.

'Hey,' she said, grabbing my face and redirecting my attention. 'What are you thinking about?'

'Sorry.'

'What was so important that stopped you from listening to me,' she said playfully.

'Umm, well.'

'Never mind, I'll take your distraction as a compliment.'

I smiled and gathered my composure. I took a sip of the coffee and bit into a croissant.

'I asked about your childhood,' she said.

'To be honest, I don't remember much about it,' I replied.

'That bad?'

'It wasn't much fun. I tried to forget most of it, but I have *some* good memories. The days I worked with my uncle on the farm, playing with the dogs, running through the ploughed dirt with cap guns in hand, firing off shots. It drove the dogs up the wall. They'd try to tear the guns out of my hands. I'd stay out until the sun disappeared and Mum's yelling became louder and more urgent. That was the worst time, going home.'

'What was so bad about home?'

'In the fields, I could imagine all sorts of things. But home was different. I remember it was crowded and scary. My father loathed me, and the fear was conjured,' I said, looking into the coffee that was as murky as those childhood memories.

On hearing my father's car pull up, the heavy footsteps of steel-capped workbooks hit the stairs and the landing. The squeak of the old brass door handle and the bottom half of the barn-style door swinging open, crashing into the wall. It had been buried there so many times a perfectly shaped dint welcomed the knob like a catcher's mitt. I remember having a better relationship with the living room floor than my father. When my father entered the room, I kept low, quiet and hidden; maybe he wouldn't notice me. The worst days were when he'd stopped off for more than a few drinks at the pub. I knew when it was one of those days. The smell of old brew and a cold chill filled the air, sucking the life out of the room. I imagined that's how space felt like—cold, silent, crushing. But I'd take that fear anytime over the belt. It became really interesting when he was so drunk, he couldn't tell the difference between the strap and buckle.

'I'm sorry, I shouldn't have said anything,' I said, reacting to her stunned silence. 'I never talk about my childhood with anyone.'

'No, I want to know,' she responded, cradling my face and easing the visible pain. 'I would never have known you'd been through something like that and come out the way you did.'

'You think I'm strong,' I said. 'Perhaps I am strong enough to pick you up.'

'No, no, don't,' she said with a shrilled laugh, using her hands to stop my advances.

'Not keen to play?'

'Time for play is over, well, for the moment anyway. It's time for other things. I must take care of a few urgent things at the office.'

I touched her face and kissed her gently on the cheek.

'I love you,' I whispered.

'I know you do.'

Letitia paused a moment and looked into my eyes.

'I need to make some decisions,' she said. 'I'm going home to talk with my parents. I've told my mum about you and what's been happening here. I can't keep putting this off, and I hoped it would work out. Do you understand?'

I did, more than she realised. I wanted her to know how much I understood the decision she had to make. Stay in the marriage, try one more time, or admit it is over and make the break once and for all. Maintaining contact with her husband and trying to help him through the separation would no longer work.

'No matter what happens with us in the future,' I said, 'if you need more time and space to make your marriage work, then I understand. I'll take a step back and honour your wishes.'

'But what if it takes a year or more for us to be together,' she said. 'I'd understand if that is too long for you to wait.'

'I'll wait, I promise. I'm not going anywhere. I love you.'

I wanted to yell, '*Choose me, not him*', but I didn't. It wasn't right to force her to do anything. I knew what it took to walk away from a marriage. Plus, she had to consider her family and what a failed marriage meant for them. Even though I knew this, I wanted to be selfish but couldn't. I reluctantly let go of her hand, and she headed for the door and the rest of her day.

PART FOUR

CHAPTER 17

A field of tall spear grass stretched out almost to the cliff's edge, overlooking the house, the valley and the bay beyond. The monsoonal 'knock-em-down' storms that would sweep across the mountain range, flattening the grass, were a month or more away. I watched my mother's palms caress the waist-high bulbous seeds, arching the stems eastward to the bay until snapping back to regimented attention. We sat at the cliff's edge, and I wrapped my arms around her waist and hugged her tightly.

'Is everything ok?' mother whispered.

'No, not really, but it will be,' I said.

She lightly touched my hair, sliding gently around to cup my face. Her gaze rested intently into my eyes.

'You have been so quiet since you arrived. We are worried.'

'Sorry,' I responded. 'I need to talk with you.'

'You're so upset when you talk with him. Is it about what happened?'

'Yes and no,' I replied. 'It can't go on like this. I need your help to talk with Papa. He won't understand what I am about to do.'

'It's ok. Papa will, now he knows what that man is like. I'm so sorry. I should have listened to you sooner.'

'Did Papa say anything to you?'

'No, not a word. He just sat under the mango tree, looking out to the bay. I asked if he was ok. But he just shrugged his shoulders.'

I'd like to think what Papa saw would make him understand, but he was caught between guilt and betrayal. He knew there was no chance of reconciliation, but what would people think of him and the family? These were powerful pulls, and no matter how much he wanted to protect me, commitment, even one laced with irony, had a firm hold on him.

I sent messages to Jack. One was a video of my mother walking among the spear grass, and then another.

It's quiet here, so peaceful. I've had a lot of time to think about everything and decide. I'm flying home tomorrow.

It was late in the afternoon when the phone rang again—the call made for a welcome relief. Heavy rain had swept quickly over the island, with its departure summoning the heat as the moisture searched for a path back to the heavens.

'Did you see the video?' I asked Jack.

'Walking through the field?' he responded. 'Is that close to your home?'

'Yes, but it's a steep climb to the top of the mountain. But from there, you can see the whole bay. I'd love to bring you here.'

'I'd like nothing more.'

'Mum and I often walk here late in the afternoon. It's always so peaceful. I told her about us, about you. I'll show you the view from up here when we visit.'

It was no longer just about her and what she needed to do but now what *we* would do. Going home had flipped the switch.

'Look, you need to know something,' I said tentatively. 'It's important that we're honest with each other.'

'Always, what's going on?'

'My husband turned up the other night.'

My heart sank. Unexpected and unannounced, but full of promises and charm. Not for Letitia but for her parents. Winning them over would help leverage support for a reunion. He pleaded for forgiveness and promised to change and be a better husband.

'I couldn't believe he just turned up,' I said. 'I told him it was over.'

My voice quivered.

'Then he started with the threats again. First at me, then you. I know he was the person who sent those letters. The same things he said in them, he said to me, word-for-word. He'd leave me without a home or family and get you fired, and I wouldn't have you. My family would disown me. I'd have no one, no man. I said I didn't need a man. But I'm not going to stop seeing you.'

It wasn't what she said, but the tension in her voice. If she was right and he'd written the letters, this wouldn't stop because she'd told him no. She didn't want to admit it, but he had become more desperate. He'd controlled her life and monitored every move she made, following her, spying on her. That wouldn't stop, not until he had control again. For now, he had none and that made him desperate.

Perhaps she was right about the park. Did he know the end would come sooner than he'd thought possible? Was this his last play to win her back? He couldn't have read her texts. Or was there something else? After all that'd happened, she didn't owe her husband anything. He'd used her generosity to stay close enough to be part of her life. He'd done it before, and he would undoubtedly do it again. I breathed deeply.

'I have to tell you something else, and you're gonna get mad, but please don't,' she pleaded.

I couldn't guarantee that.

CHAPTER 18

For the first time, I'd slipped effortlessly into a peaceful sleep. I dreamed of a life with a man I could trust, who loved me and wanted everything for me. Everything was now possible, and I swam further into the shallows, protected from the tumult of my chaotic life.

I couldn't remember what woke me. Maybe it was a sense of something else in an almost pitch-black room. I dismissed the feeling as a lingering essence of my heightened alert to the months of hostile text messages. I should've listened.

I felt a knee press hard against the back of my neck. I struggled to breathe, and only the searing pain in my shoulder kept me from losing consciousness. He'd pinned my wrist with his left hand, leaving his right free. He leaned over, stroking my face like a romantic gesture. It wasn't. He shanked at my hair, and my neck crunched loudly.

'You're mine, and I'll do what I want with you,' he growled in my ear.

I felt his breath cling to my face, heavy with the smell of bourbon. It comforted his anger, fuelled his rage, and encouraged his daring. I struggled more, welcoming the pain if it would free me, even a little. Each surge of pain, each twinge, kept me conscious. I bared down on it. I kicked out with my free legs but couldn't find the target I had searched for in the dark. I knew what I had to do. Struggle more, stay conscious, call out. But the pressure on my neck cut off more than just air, stopping any chance to be heard. In the next room, her parents lay asleep. He reached down with his free hand and yanked at my underwear, tearing them, exposing me to his will. He inserted his finger. I screamed in pain. But it was barely audible.

He moved. It released the pressure from my neck momentarily, but I was still pinned, weakened, and exposed to his wanton desire. I felt him. Hard. It was now or never. I wasn't going to be raped. Not by him. Not by anyone. I pushed up as much as possible with my free hand to leverage even the smallest space. It freed me, and I took a deep breath, enough to get some air in my lungs to scream and be heard. But he felt me move and applied more pressure on my arm. I struggled as much as I could as he rode up against me, trying to push himself inside.

I clenched every muscle in my body, shutting down his advance. He pushed even harder into me. I clenched even tighter. He rocked back and forth, trying to pierce my resolve. I felt his frustration and anger. He let go of my wrist and grabbed a handful of hair. He pulled hard, then slammed my face into the pillow. My arm ached, but it was free. No blood flow, no feeling. I rolled my shoulder and managed to move it, but my arm fell limply down the side of the bed. I pulled my left leg up and rolled to the side as he rocked back. It was enough to tip him ever so slightly. He tried to recover, but the alcohol took control. His hand searched for the edge of the bed, but he missed in the darkness. He crashed heavily to the floor, slamming his head on the carved wooden duchess.

Now free, I rolled over and reached for the lamp beside the bed. Some feeling returned to my arm, but my fingers were still numb. I fumbled with the switch. The lamp toppled to the floor with a flurry of light swivelling around the room, startling him. I couldn't see him, but I heard his moans. I backed up against the bed head. I pulled my legs against my chest, wrapping both arms around them. My underwear dangled from one bent knee like a flag at half-mast. But there was no surrender. I felt tears roll down my face, and I wiped them away. He'd get no satisfaction from seeing my pain and fear. I could hear movement from the floor at the bottom of the bed. I swivelled at the edge, and my feet hit the carpet. A whale lay beached on the floor, flailing, hand covering a gash on his left forehead. Blood oozed through his fingers.

He looked up, and I saw defeat. The most logical option would be to quit. He grabbed the corner of the bed, but his blooded fingers slipped, and he crashed back to the floor.

In the doorway, my parents stood silently. They hadn't seen the attack, only the aftermath. They looked at me in disbelief and *guilt-ridden*. Embarrassed and still bleeding, he lifted himself to his feet, trying to pull his pants up as he grasped for the bed. He cast his eyes downward and said nothing as he passed by my parents. What could he say?

By morning, he was gone. So was the veneer of respect Mumma and Papa once had for him and our marriage.

CHAPTER 19

'Are you ok?' I asked.

I had no real way of understanding how she felt. How could I?

'Yes, no, maybe,' Letitia's voice cracked. 'I'm not sure, but I'm still in shock. He's never done that before. Threats, yes, but that, no.'

'You have to report him to the police.'

'I can't,' she said.

'Why? He tried to rape you.'

'It's my word against his. The police won't take it seriously. They never do. They'll think he has the right as my husband.'

'No one has that right,' I protested.

'It happens all the time. Most police are men, so they take the man's side every time.'

'Aren't there women police officers in the villages now?'

'Yes, but not nearly enough. And even if they make a report, it must go through to the higher-ranked male police officers, and it'll go no further. Change happens slowly here, unfortunately. But I'm one of the lucky ones, and most women don't survive these attacks.'

'It's not right,' I said. 'No matter the situation, there's no excusing that.'

'No, there's not,' Letitia agreed. 'He's already sent texts apologising, blaming the alcohol. He tried to call, but I didn't pick up. I don't want to speak to him.'

'Use the texts as proof,' I responded, pushing the issue.

'He didn't say what he did, so there's no proof to show. He's smart enough not to.'

'But dumb enough to try,' I responded.

'Agree, but at least my parents, mostly Papa, know what he's like now.'

I sensed no chance of convincing her to report the attack, so I relented and took a different tack.

'When are you back?' I asked.

'Thursday afternoon, just in time for the writing competition. The Poetry Slam is on.'

'What's a Poetry Slam?' I said.

'You've never heard of a Slam?'

'New to me.'

'You haven't seen the posters plastered all over campus?'

'I don't usually take much notice with the boards pinned with notices over notices.'

'Every year, the school stages a writing competition,' Letitia explained. 'It's a big deal with people presenting their poetry or short stories about various topics.'

'Just students?' I asked.

'No, some lecturers present their latest work or use it as a test-run for their ideas. Haven't you ever entered a writing competition?'

'Of course, once, but it's been a while.'

'Did you win?'

'Of course, I won,' I responded.

'Like money or something?'

'A Walkley, much like the Pulitzer.'

'That's good then,' she said. 'Anyway, they make all the entrants get up and read what they've written.'

'What the hell has that got to do with writing?' I said. 'Writers write, and readers read. Right? That makes no sense to me. Let someone else read it.'

'Have you read anything that you've written to anyone?

'Like in public? I can barely read what I write in private and never out loud. And certainly not to people I don't know. I'm too shy for that. I want the reading of my work to remain a mystery to me.'

'You shy?' she said. 'I find that hard to believe.'

'So, it's like that coffee shop reading shit they go on with,' I said. 'The writer comes in, signs a few books, and reads a passage to an adoring crowd.'

'I hadn't thought of it that way.'

'You know why writers do that kind of bullshit?'

'Sell books, I guess.'

'Hell no, they do it to get laid.'

'Seriously, people will sleep with you if you write a book?'

'People will sleep with you if you write a bad book.'

'Did that ever happen to you?'

'Of course.'

'So, I'm guessing that's no to the Slam.'

'Hell no, I'll be there. A chance to see students squirm under pressure. Wouldn't miss it for the world.'

'You're sick.'

'Oh no, it's about the spectacle, you know, to support the greater learning community.'

'Yeah, right,' Letitia responded.

The call ended. I returned to the office from the radio studios on the hill overlooking the campus. As I walked along the path and passed several buildings, slam posters came into full view, pinned haphazardly to noticeboards, light poles, and the sides of buildings. It seemed like they'd sprung up overnight. Each bulletin board was covered with not one but a squadron of flyers, announcing 'Come Slam with Slam!'. The boards were never cleaned despite a sign reading 'Remove the notices, not this sign'. The irony of a sign unread was not lost among the groaning weight of papier-mâché past, present and future events.

I grabbed one of the flyers as I walked to the writing lab. The venue was new to me. My travels had been limited to the gym, office, lecture theatre, and coffee shop. A 7pm start, it read, so arriving 30 minutes late would snare a good spot for the show's beginning.

I could have looked on the campus map for the venue, but I decided local knowledge would be quicker.

'Hey, Priya! Got a minute?' I yelled, interrupting the student's frantic typing.

'Yes, sir,' she said as she leaned toward the office's open door.

'Are you going to the Poetry Slam?'

'Of course,' she said. 'I think I'm third or fourth on the schedule. But I need to get this story done and submitted for the paper.'

'Good, good, where is the Performance Centre?'

'West of the administration building.'

Getting instructions with references to compass settings was of little help. Priya noticed my confusion.

'It's the large fancy building between the campus Administration Office and the No.1 Food Stall,' she added.

'Better, I know the one. See you tonight.'

She retreated to her story and the pressure of the deadline.

I wanted to go home for my afternoon nap, but the heavens prevented my escape.

CHAPTER 20

The Performance Centre was built as a creative space but felt like a small airport hangar. A large, hollowed structure with two entrances on either side of the building offered access, but only one for ticketholders. The other doorway led to a courtyard where food and refreshments waited on two collapsible tables. It wasn't fancy and didn't need to be. A table for wine and beers and another for sandwiches and snacks kept the event casual. A seven-tier steel bleacher rose against the back wall, with a small stage partly filling the right-hand corner at the other end. Three collapsible chairs for judges and a microphone stood at the centre of the space. It was untethered from the performers seated next to the stage. They may have sat together but were alone, each struggling desperately in a sea of anxiety.

I was late, but so was everyone else. I found a spot without being noticed. That's a tough ask if you're the only one of the few foreigners in the building. Sitting in the bleachers was not an option – far too exposed. I opted for one of three seats resting against the wall close to the main door entrance, performers, and an easy escape. It was a good and clever plan until it wasn't. There were just too many spare seats.

'Hi sir,' came a voice from the doorway.

I didn't have to look around to see who it was. I recognised the gravelled voice and was pleased it was her. She eased into the seat.

'Your virgin slam,' Kat said.

No matter how often we interreacted, my first thought was never to call her by her name, though politeness ruled my response. She would always be 'student forty-one' – the non-submission, non-submissive. I liked that about her. A familiarity of mischievousness that thumbed one's nose at deadlines and rules. These were traits I admired but that I kept to myself. I didn't sense any suggestion of flirting, but I wasn't sure what others would think if they overheard the conversation. But that mattered little. Control what you can control.

'Yes,' I said with a wry smile. 'Hopefully, they'll be gentle with me.'

'I think you're in for a treat,' she responded. 'Slams get pretty interesting.'

I was polite enough not to voice my doubts. But I wasn't here for that anyway; it would be a bonus if it were so. I felt comfortable now, much more than I would typically for such a first-time event. The exchange distracted me from the sudden surge of people at the performers' end of the space. Judges mingled around the desk, and the Master of Ceremonies tapped the mic and welcomed the audience.

'I'm Johnny Namesake, Johnny Namesake's my name,' the Emcee launched into a rap to set the tone of the evening. 'If all your names were Johnny Namesake, then all our names would be the same,' he trailed off to the cheers and laughter from the audience.

That was unexpected. Maybe it would be fun after all. It was a definite break from the stuffy veneer of poetry's traditional format and seemed to connect with the audience.

'Here's a little history for those new to a Poetry Slam,' he said as his eyes surveyed the room, landing uncomfortably on me. 'It all started 30 years ago in America to trick people into coming to poetry events by putting an exciting word like 'slam' at the end. We've got an excellent line-up of experienced and novice performers tonight. So, let's make them welcome because I'm sure a few are a little nervous. And please remember that you, the audience, make this event special for budding poets and performers.'

I glanced at the gaggle seated in the shadowed corner of the space. There was some idle chit-chat but mostly intense silence. Each performer focused on their notes, mouthing intro lines and scribbling some last-minute changes. The hope, I expect, was that maybe the changes would make a difference. True to its heritage, the list of performances deviated from its elitist core. It promised to be loud and irreverent. They had three minutes, and all performers had to adhere to the tight schedule. The Emcee interjected if they didn't comply, and the audience would heckle. It was loud and lively, and the audience loved it, even when a runner thrust a piece of white cardboard and a thick-tipped Sharpie pen into my hand. I offered no resistance, accepting my part in the performance.

'See, I said it would be interesting,' Kat whispered.

I held up the card with a circled figure.

'What do we have here,' the Emcee yelled. 'Professor, it's an eight, or the highest score ever seen in a poetry slam.'

So much for anonymity, as I peered over the card to see an infinity symbol floating ambiguously on the card.

'No, no, definitely an eight,' I yelled, turning the card to the side and showing it to the judges and the audience, who dismissed the lower-than-anticipated score.

'No,' yelled an audience member from the top of the bleachers.

A friend of the performer, perhaps.

'Give him the higher score. He deserves it for that performance,' another voice echoed from the other end of the bleachers.

It was a voice I knew, and I looked up and smiled. It lingered longer than a casual acquittance. Letitia smiled back.

'Win some, lose some,' the Emcee responded with a shrug.

The next performer was invited on stage, and the tempo continued. A small woman sprung to her feet and rushed out of the darkness, grabbing the mic, delighted with her chance to lay down her lyrics and beatbox. She launched into a solo, 'Island Feet'.

As performers rolled through the schedule, the crowd became louder. Each performer's name and score were added to the tally board. But the judges' scores were yet to come. After a few minutes of quick consultation, the Emcee walked to the mic and stood still as the crowd quietened. Only a few whispers were heard from the top of the bleachers.

Glances from the Emcee and a few shushes from the gallery silenced those quickly.

'Before we crown the slam champ, let me first thank you all for your wonderful participation and support,' the Emcee said. 'What makes this so different is the competitive nature of all those here, performers and audience members alike. Everyone has done an incredible job tonight, but there must be a winner.'

'Come on,' an impatient voice yelled from the stands. 'Tell us my friend won, ok.'

People erupted into cheers. The Emcee smiled and gestured towards the bleachers to calm the audience.

'Perhaps you could present next year, Stephen,' the Emcee said, making the young man shrink into the recesses of the crowd. 'So, the winner tonight can call themselves the King or Queen of Slam and bask in your fifteen minutes. If you lose tonight, dismiss poetry as subjective art and claim you can't put numbers on creativity. So, let's congratulate political science student Eliki Tikoidraubuta for his poem *What is it Like to be a Real Fijian Man*? Let's hear it for Eliki!'

Most cheered, and some booed expectantly, but those were quickly drowned out. I felt a hard pull on my forearm. Kat pointed to the far end of the bleachers where Letitia sat with two students I recognised.

'Let's go,' she said, pulling me towards the group.

I offered no resistance.

'Hi, everyone,' I said, sitting on the same level as the students, just below Letitia.

'Do you know everyone, Stephen and Samuel?' Letitia asked.

'I know Stephan quite well. But Samuel and I haven't interacted much in class. But we know each other, right?'

Samuel nodded. I leaned over and shook both their hands. Samuel may not have said much in class, but his work impressed lecturers and tutors alike. None more than Letitia, who'd talked about him often and with considerable admiration. It took much to impress her, and she rejoiced in his writing skill as much as his quiet charm. I, too, had taken delight in his creative writing, none more so than his obituary a few weeks earlier.

It came to light through that creative lens how an Indo-Fijian boy had drawn his name from the Old Testament. It seemed appropriate. He'd made his pilgrimage from the outer part of the big island for learning and knowledge. His shyness came from a life of sheltered experiences, with his family hailing from Ba in the northwest. Like many, he was not a progeny of richness. His decedents had carved out a living growing sugar cane, not more than a stone's throw from the local mill. As is often true of those from the sweet country, hard work turned toil into prominence. I could relate to such humble beginnings.

Samuel's good looks matched the charm when he spoke. His blue-green eyes were a quirk of nature or maybe a lineage crossed. When he relaxed, one eye wandered outward just a little. He was not a lean man but delicate, nonetheless. His palms were uncalloused and soft, not of someone who'd worked the sugar fields, unlike his grandfather. But neither was his father, who had seen a brighter future for his family in mercantile, moving the family to Nadi to start a small business with his older brother. The move provided other opportunities that the hard labour fields could not. Over time, that commitment secured considerable financial gains and a position in the community. But what set Samuel apart from other family members was being the first in the family to attend university. That uniqueness brought pressure to succeed. Perhaps that alone was enough to see something special in the young man.

'Are you all in Letitia's class too?' I asked.

Samuel smiled and looked up at her. His reverence was palpable; she was popular with students and faculty.

'Hey, Prof, sorry about the other day in class,' Stephen interjected.

'Did you take my advice and look up Stein?'

'No, I already knew of her and was just joking around. Apologies.'

'Don't apologise,' I insisted. 'It was funny.'

Stephen smiled. But Letitia wasn't about to let that one slide.

'Let us in on the joke,' she enquired.

'You had to be there,' Stephen responded quickly, avoiding revisiting his moment of classroom notoriety.

'I guess so,' Letitia said with a shrug of disappointment.

A movement near the doorway caught my attention. A man stood, staring at the group from the dark recesses just beyond the entrance. A rotund figure, almost obese, with a solemn look of distrust and a large gauze Band-Aid covering a gash above his left eye. He quickly looked away and moved far enough out of sight. Letitia leaned across, close enough for me to hear but not the others.

'Don't take any notice of him,' she whispered, directing my attention away from the doorway.

Outside, the man returned, arms folded. The look had now changed. There was a mix of fear and anger directed at how comfortable Letitia was with me, and she was no longer hiding her feelings. But I struggled with why he was here after what had happened a few days ago.

'He was at the airport,' Letitia explained. 'I couldn't get rid of him, and he just invited himself along. Sorry.'

I ignored him and relaxed against the steel bleacher. But the gesture didn't go unnoticed, with the students looking around to see what had grabbed my attention.

'So, what did you think of the presentations,' I said, drawing them back to the group.

'I think it was one of our best slams,' Samuel said.

'Good to see staff supporting our slamming,' Stephen chimed in.

'What did *you* think of the slam, Prof?' Kat said.

'It's my first one, so it's all a bit new to me,' I said, hoping to offset further focus on Letitia's husband.

'The doc's not a fan of poetry,' Letitia interrupted.

'Oh really?' Samuel said.

'Ok, let me clarify that,' I said, sounding defensive and slightly embarrassed. 'It's courageous of the performers to get up in front of their peers and present their work.'

'That's a little condescending, isn't it?' Kat said with a familiarity that surprised the others, including Letitia. 'I heard you say poetry is like comedy without the punchline.'

'Oh, wow, you don't think much of it,' Stephen said.

'Well, I think that was presumptive of me,' I responded. 'Maybe I'm a little embarrassed that I'm not good at poetry, and perhaps it is a little too esoteric for me. After seeing the performances, I think I'll revise my assessment.'

'Well, we can't be good at all writing,' Kat said. 'Did you like any of the presentations?'

'I did,' I said. 'The one on languages is something I know a little about.'

'It's a sensitive topic here,' Stephen said. 'You'll get a very different response on language, depending on who you talk to.'

I had enough working knowledge of the trap many Westerners fall into. I'd listened and learned quickly. I knew the rules that governed multiculturalism on the islands. Each one had its intricacies and exposed subtle fault lines. My experiences and all that I'd reaped over time were enough to know the power of language to shape and influence perceptions. That, too, could be equally said of religion. These two lived symbiotic truths on the islands. But such power does not reside in the language or religion. It resides in those who harness and wield its influence in their favour. That was no more evident than in how both had been politicised and exercised to curate an identity that would hopefully transcend long-held prejudices that panged islanders.

'So, how do you define yourselves, Indo-Fijians or Fijians?' I went fishing with a loaded response.

'We are Fijians,' Letitia corrected me. 'We don't identify as ethnic groups. That term separates, not harmonises us. We've struggled enough with that dilemma.'

'Correct me if I am wrong, but Fijians of Indian descent speak Hindustani, yes?' I asked, taking care to construct the question sensitively.

'Correct,' Stephan said. 'But only with others who speak Hindi, mostly at home or with a friend. Or perhaps shopping at specific businesses.'

'So, what do you think the presenter was saying?' I asked.

'That we can speak our language and still be Fijian,' Samuel said, breaking his silence.

'Language does not define us but identifies us,' Letitia added.

'Do you all believe that?' I asked.

'I believe you're trying to see whether what we say, think, and value come under the one broad cultural banner,' Kat responded perceptively, characterising her intellect.

'I guess God is in the detail,' I replied, smiling.

'Don't you mean the Devil is in the detail?' Stephen asked.

'Depends on whether you see language as malign or benign,' I said.

'How so?' Letitia responded.

'Ok, if you believe that God is in the detail, then you believe in the wonder of His creation, in this case, language, as a defining positive aspect of people's lives and look for what is good,' I said. 'If you believe that the Devil is in the detail, you see something negative, a deception. Which one fits your way of thinking?'

'I think you'd get overwhelming support for God here given the majority Christian population,' Letitia said.

'But this is a multicultural society made of Christians, Muslims and Hindus,' I offered. 'As much as language is a defining aspect of culture, so is religion.'

'Yes, but some things are valued more, and religion is one of those,' Samuel said.

'Why is that?' I enquired.

'Because here God is always in the detail,' said Stephen with his trademark smile of mischievousness.

I smiled along, and the others laughed. It drew looks from those lingering in the space and outside. It would have been easy to dismiss Stephen as the class clown. But there was more to him. He wasn't afraid to say what he thought. His humour and wit were contagious. A playfulness that drew you to him like an alluring light in the darkness. Stephen challenged me, and I liked that.

'We're heading off to watch the football at a pub in the city,' Letitia said. 'Do you want to come with us?'

'I think threes a crowd,' I said, glancing to the open door where her husband still lingered outside silently with arms folded.

'He's not coming,' Letitia said. 'Only Ravi, Samuel and a few others are going. Come along. It'll be fun.'

'Thank you,' I said. 'I'm pretty whacked. It's been a huge week, and I need a good sleep. Plus, there's plenty of time for that come tomorrow.'

Letitia leaned close to me.

'See you at 8am,' she whispered.

I smiled and nodded.

'Enjoy your night, and be safe,' I said, glancing gently at Letitia.

CHAPTER 21

I waited until 8am as we'd planned. Phone calls and texts went unanswered. Hours went by, each one adding to my concern. I knew something was wrong. But I couldn't go to her house. I searched Letitia's Facebook page until I found her mother's contact. It was a long shot, but I had to try something. Concern had grown to fear.

'You may not want to hear from me,' I wrote in the message. 'But I am worried about Letitia. Have you heard from her today?'

I waited, expecting no reply. I was the last person her mother wanted to hear from, but I was wrong.

'Hello,' the response came almost immediately. 'No, I called her, but she did not respond.'

'Have you tried to contact her husband?' I asked MummaG.

'Yes, I spoke with him early this morning,' she wrote back. 'He said everything was alright and she'd call soon.'

But Letitia didn't call. Her concern matched mine. She spoke with her daughter at least once a day, sometimes more. A call to say hello, ask how she was, whether she had made an appointment for her father at the hospital, and what she was cooking for dinner. These moments were nothing-and-everything conversations. I could wait no longer. I went in search of the person Letitia confided in most. I arrived at Esther's campus office and asked to see her. Her assistant asked me to make an appointment, but I insisted it was urgent. It may have been the concern in my voice or the look on my face.

'I'm Jack, Letitia's friend,' I said, extending my hand to Letitia's psychiatrist.

'It is nice to meet you,' Esther said, offering the seat opposite her. 'It feels like I already know you.'

'Oh, why?'

'Letitia spoke of you often and at length. You've become close.'

'That's why I am here,' I said, 'she was supposed to come to the apartment yesterday morning, and I can't contact her.'

'She's not responding to your texts or calls?'

'No, and her mother is worried too.'

'You spoke with her mother?' Esther said, surprised by the contact. 'I spoke with Letitia on Monday, and she was so excited about her decision and plans.'

She called Letitia's number, but there was no answer. She texted, but nothing came back.

'That worries me,' Esther said. 'I'll head over to her house.'

I watched as Esther called a taxi and packed up. We left the building together and waited for the car to arrive.

'I'll call you as soon as I arrive at the house, ok?'

I nodded and headed across campus and home.

I watched Esther enter the taxi and saw her make another call.

CHAPTER 22

'I am worried about one of my students. I'm heading to her home now. Would it be possible to send someone to meet me there?'

I arrived a few minutes before a police car pulled beside the taxi. I knocked on the front door, but no answer. I retreated to the property's front gate and waited for the police car, which pulled up just a few minutes later.

'I knocked on the door. I can hear the television from inside the house,' I said to the two police officers as they approached her.

The female police officer spoke first.

'We'll look and see if we can get a response,' the officer said.

'Do you think something has happened?' the more senior male officer asked.

'I don't know, but she hasn't responded to calls and texts from people, including her mother, so I am worried.'

'Have there been problems between her and the husband before?' The female offered asked.

'Nothing violent that I know of, but Letitia mentioned something that happened a few days ago but didn't go into detail,' I said. 'She's spoken about his jealousy and harassing calls and texts. I am worried.'

The male officer peered through the slits of the louvred windows at the side of the building. A man lay motionless in a chair in front of the television, a bottle of gin empty and smashed glass on the floor.

I watched as the police smashed their way into the home through the side door. Its single lock blew out quickly, and the door flung open, hitting hard against the cupboard that cornered the kitchen. Splinters of glass panels in the door crashed to the floor. That would have usually raised attention, but there was no response within the house. Half sitting, half reclining, Letitia's husband's lifeless body lay contorted on the seat. Arms stretched to the floor, streams of life, now hardened, pooled over the broken glass and floorboards below his sliced wrists.

Police checked for a pulse as a matter of finality. They searched for Letitia. Opening the door to the main bedroom, they found clothes strewn across the floor and a mattress overturned, but no one. They moved to the spare bedroom. The officers' gasps reverberated through the house and beyond.

The razor-sharp meat cleaver had done what it was designed to do, and a deep pool of blood arched around her body. It seemed nothing had changed, just the choice of blade, with men holding women to ransom under the razor-sharp edges of cane knives, a way to instil fear and control. Her face was so beautiful and angelic in life, now frozen, her eyes open, pleading for mercy or searching for a reason, and her mouth was slack. Her body was made immobile by a coward's jealousy. Her eternal warmth of the ages he said he loved was now gone.

Flashes would capture the scene in horrific detail. He'd not just killed Letitia but humiliated her. The rope, new and twisted ligatures that strengthened its hold, was embedded in her wrists and ankles— trussed like an animal to slaughter. She'd struggled and fought, which only tightened the grip as the knotted rope followed its design logic. She was at his mercy, and none was given.

CHAPTER 23

The call came an hour later. I rushed back to Esther's office. I didn't want to imagine the worst, but thoughts seeped through that weakened veneer. It had only been an hour. It would have taken Esther that long to get to the house and back to her office. If Letitia weren't there, locating her would only take a little longer. But deep in the recesses of my soul, there was a quickening of fear I didn't want to consider. What if?

Esther stood at the rigid in the office doorway. Her face offered no expression, no indication of what her search had revealed. Or was it something else? Her professional tonality slowly waivered, and a solemn tear slipped past her professional veneer. I was frozen in fear as my mind tried desperately to untangle inevitability from possibility. Moans escaped her lips through the suppressed sound of fortified weeping.

'I'm so sorry,' Esther said, trying desperately to control the uncontrollable. 'She's gone.'

'What do you mean?' I pleaded. 'Where has she gone.'

'No, Jack,' Esther replied, holding my trembling hand. 'She's no longer with us. It is awful, and I am so sorry.'

The pounding in my chest beat a cold, lifeless rhythm as the horrifying truth seeped through my disbelief. I stepped out into the bright sunlight and looked out over the campus. I knew if I walked past my office and through the hallways, someone would notice me and ask what was wrong. I just couldn't face that. I turned and weaved through the student and staff housing to the back gate. It was mid-morning, and only a few people were around, but none I knew. I passed through the entrance. There was no guard. The feeder street led to the main road and the ocean's edge. I stood looking out into the vast expanse. I tried to process it all, but instead, it consumed me. I didn't want to go home only to be reminded of her lingering presence and the expectancy of her commitment to me, now forever gone.

I don't remember much after that, only realising I was sitting on a downtown curbside, like a homeless man without hope cast into a lonely wind. People passed by, and I sensed their downcast looks as I covered my face, now buried in my huddled thighs, circled tightly with my arms, trying desperately to shut out a world too ugly to imagine.

'Brother,' Davis's voice reverberated down the line.

The low rumble comforted me but was as brief as the call. Davis waited for an answer that never came.

'Are you okay?'

'No,' my voice crumbled.

'Where are you?

'Across from Onyx. I don't know how I got here. I just don't know.'

Passing cars and conversations of people moving to the next round of Friday night drinks muffled the reply.

'Stay there. I'm coming to you.'

The phone went dead. I'd heard every word but couldn't remember any of them. I couldn't move even if I wanted to. Time slowed, and everything around me disappeared as I drowned in the chaotic silence. I could only feel the intense pounding of my broken heart. I pushed back against a light post, fortifying myself from the growing darkness outside and within. I could only think of one thing.

A voice came from above. Davis's large hands hoisted me, and I fell into his cavernous embrace.

'I know what happened,' Davis said solemnly. 'Esther called me. You wouldn't answer her calls. She was worried about you. I am so, so sorry, brother.'

'I can't feel anything, nothing,' I responded feebly. 'She's not here anymore. Why?'

'I can't answer that, my friend,' Davis responded, searching for anything to say that could cushion the fall. 'I'm taking you to Sonja's house, where her husband and Ravi are waiting for us. We're all here for you.'

I remember the tears, the hugs, and the murmured conversations from the lounge room. I listened intently as sleep was not an option. I didn't want to imagine what had happened, but I could make out the conversation's incoherent ramblings. But some things resonated more cogently.

'I don't think he should go to the funeral,' I heard Ravi say.

'What did Leti's mother say?' Sonja asked.

'We haven't discussed it with her,' said Ravi. 'It's up to her and only her.'

'I think he'll want to go for some closure, don't you think?' Davis asked. 'Maybe Jack should contact her and ask if it is ok to attend.'

'I don't think that's a good idea,' Ravi said. 'She just lost her daughter and may blame him for what has happened.'

'He's not to blame for this,' Davis responded.

'No,' Ravi replied. 'But such a rational response may not be something she can muster right now.'

'Let's see if Jack wants to go first,' Sonja interrupted. 'We can worry about how that plays out with the family later.'

I don't remember falling asleep. I listened to the door creak twice as Sonja and her husband checked on me. They'd done their duty and watched over me during the night. I knew what they were thinking, but something profound inside me couldn't contemplate such thoughts.

No one moved into the apartment, and I didn't want to disturb them. The light outside was weak and empty.

Journal

Date: 22 July 2012

Letitia,

There isn't a minute of my life without you in it. I write the words and construct the passages, and all the while, the memories come flooding in like the tide lapping against the stone wall of Apted Park. Inevitable and relentless.

I was thinking today that when you left my world for another, I was much more frightened than I would possibly admit. I fought my fears by telling myself I would see you again someday. And I thought about what I would say to you. I must have written a hundred possibilities, but I found none worthy to say. My mouth would not work except to feel your lips upon mine. And when you said you'd be waiting for me, it said it all.

Well, I'm doing it again. I wonder what I'll say to you when I see you again. I think of that every day, unwilling to let go and join you but willingly embracing the possibilities when that inevitability arrives at my moment of mortality.

Jack.

CHAPTER 24

MummaG approached the funeral pyre and the yellow-wrapped body of the daughter she longed to hug one more time. Her tears stained her round, contorted face, and no amount of wiping could remove that pain, not now, not in a year, never. All around was a sad blur of activity. Men lighting the fire around the body, feet first, her younger brother circling the pyre and casting holy water onto Letitia's body, chanting prayers lingered in the heavy air.

I stood with Ravi and Sonja. I felt eyes upon me. No one said anything to me, but the murmurs were loud and clear. Perhaps this was a mistake, and I wanted to retreat. As my weight shifted, a hand reached out found my elbow and squeezed a fortifying embrace. I looked to my left, and Sonja gestured to the hill overlooking the funeral pyre, a green sweep of the incline now dotted with twenty or more white-clad women. They stood in unison, arms entwined in a circle—a guard of honour or perhaps something else.

'That's something I've never seen before,' Ravi whispered.

'I thought women were not part of this ceremony, only the men,' Sonja responded.

'Not at a traditional Hindu funeral.'

'What do you make of it?' said Sonja, processing her way through the significance of the women's vigil.

'I'd say that's a protest,' Ravi replied.

'And the colour?' Sonja added.

'White means the same in Hinduism as in Western society,' Ravi said.

'Purity?' Sonja queried.

'Yes,' continued Ravi. 'Together, they're sending a strong message to men in the community.'

I'd become a frozen observer, silenced by the magnitude of what was before me. Each person bares their response to grief in different ways. I witnessed a ritual, the magnitude of which I couldn't possibly understand and a moment I would never forget.

I watched MummaG, standing at the centre of her husband and son, gaze into the pyre as the flames and the shroud became one. Letitia's earthly presence was no more, with her soul now cast out to make its heavenly ascent. She was now at peace. But the journey for those that remained had only just begun. MummaG's eyes cast to the ground. Her body was hunched, the weight of her loss crushing her soul. She stood fast, refusing to leave as her family held her. They gave her all the time she needed to accept Letitia was now gone. MummaG looked up and turned toward me. She cast aside the family, walked the twenty steps, and stood silent before me. Everyone held a collective breath. She reached up to my face, cupping it in her hands and wiped away my tears. She wrapped her arms around me and pulled me close.

'I'm so happy you came,' she whispered to me. 'You are part of my family, and I'm sorry for your loss. Please come with us.'

I couldn't answer. Even if I wanted to, I might not have found the words to say how much that meant to me. MummaG and her family returned to the bare, brick home now full of memories and loss. Photographs of Letitia's wedding remained on the sideboard. Rows of stuffed bears, some with 'I love you' stitched in red into the body, a painful memory of who had ended her daughter's beautiful life.

It was time to mourn. MummaG only left her home for a few hours and went to the Kriyaputra Bhawan and ashram for mourners to conduct the pujas. It was a place to heal. MummaG returned home each day to a place of solitude, a space created and purified where close family mourners would sleep on the floor with their heads pointing north to where Letitia's body was consumed on the pyre. Outside the home, others came and offered condolences to the family.

I watched as neighbours gathered and fed the distant relatives and visitors who were not those in deep mourning within the sanctum of the home. When MummaG and her family emerged from the house to greet us, they did not touch the ritually impure, offering privacy and space for the grieving family. She looked across at me and eked out a solemn smile.

I wondered if it was an apology or a gesture of concern for my pain. It didn't matter. There was nothing to compare a parent's loss of a child. Other extended family gathered under the shade of the large mango tree, welcoming me into their sanctuary from the heat and humidity. They fed me, supported me and eased my pain if that was indeed possible. I listened to them speak, some in English, others in Hindi. I offered little in return, just thanks to acknowledge their generosity.

So many people came and went over the next thirteen days as the family conducted ancient rituals with a rural heart.

CHAPTER 25

I swayed ever so slightly in the stiffening breeze flowing across Apted Park. Too much alcohol, but I didn't care. I hoped it would numb the pain, but it didn't. It just made me sadder than I thought possible. There was no memory of undressing and putting on shorts and a black T-shirt found crumpled at the bed's end. A quick check confirmed its worn-by date. There was no sourness, only the scent of two-day loss, with Letitia's perfume lingering within the weave. Its complex molecules clung to each thread.

There were several aborted attempts to sleep. It was maybe three, possibly more. I fumbled with the bedside lamp and started to read Vonnegut's *Slaughterhouse-Five*. I read the same pages several times. It was familiar, but it seemed new somehow. The anti-war commentary had given way to fanciful thoughts of travelling back in time. It had become an implausible reality but one I so yearned for desperately. That illusion of hope loosened the tension in my head. But I didn't want to close my eyes. The room would start spinning again. If I kept reading, that feeling would soon pass. But until then, I'd maintain the illusion of another reality.

I heard footsteps climbing the stairs, which were too loud to be one person. A crash of a closed fist slammed heavily on the steel grate.

'Police!' an officer shouted.

Maybe I was still dreaming. In the haze, I barely remembered running my hand down the four panels of the bedroom louvres the night before. I opened my eyes slowly and checked the time. It clicked to 8am with a louder-than-normal thud. I closed my eyes, rolled over, and ignored the banging outside the apartment's back door. In the semi-darkness, the future felt softer than the cold, harsh light of day already started. But the voices from the back landing grew louder, and I realised there was no escaping that destiny and returning to sleep.

'Police here,' the voice yelled. 'We need to talk with you, Professor.'

'Yes, yes, give me a moment,' I responded with frustration. 'I just woke up, and it's very early.'

'Please, we are here to ask you some questions about the incident.'

'You'll wake the neighbours if you keep banging on the door and yelling like that. I need to get dressed. Give me a minute.'

I saw two dark shapes hovering like ghostly figures through the frosted glass. As I opened the door, each officer came into sharper focus. Both wore crisp, clean uniforms, unencumbered by the day ahead. A police insignia was sewn into both arms of their light blue, short-sleeved button-down shirts. A tag hung loosely from their left chest pockets, with their names and positions easily identifiable. I took little notice. The two officers removed their berets in unison and put them under their left armpits like they'd practised a thousand times before. The senior officer introduced himself, and the younger man looked barely out of diapers, let alone police training school. Fresh-faced and an expression of eagerness that seemed out of place for the occasion.

'We need to ask you some questions regarding the murder of Ms Singh and the suicide of Mr Kumel,' the senior officer said. 'Can we come in?'

'Of course,' I said, reluctantly escorting them to the living room couch.

They both took out their police-issued leather flip notebooks and sat down. They sank uncomfortably into the floral sofa. Each squirmed a little and then moved to the edge like crows perched on a ledge. I grabbed a chair next to the French doors that led out to the balcony. It was only later that I had held the strategic high ground.

'Would you like a glass of water?' I offered politely.

'No, we are fine,' the senior officer said

'If you don't mind, I'll grab one for myself,' I suggested. 'Only be a moment.'

I poured a glass and took a long, calculated breath before consuming it in one gulp. I filled the glass again and placed it on the coffee table. Unlike the officers, I leaned back into the chair and tried to look relaxed. I wasn't, and who would be? The officers sat opposite, ready to take down every utterance and observation. Fiji police had a reputation; I wasn't about to test that now. I crossed my legs and sat silently, waiting for them to start their questioning.

'We understand you were in a relationship with Ms Singh,' the senior officer said. 'Is that correct?'

'Yes.'

'Can you tell us about your relationship with Ms Singh,' the senior officer pushed for more information.

'We met a year ago when I worked briefly at the university before working in Saudi Arabia. We talked occasionally about research and travel, things we had in common.'

'So, you were not in a relationship with her then,' the senior officer said. 'You didn't return to Fiji to continue a relationship?'

'No, and no,' I responded. 'We were friends and only spoke in my office occasionally. We never met outside of that. And the time I was away, we never communicated.'

'So, you didn't know she was married,' the senior officer pushed harder.

'No, I did not when we first started the relationship,' I said, feeling a growing concern over the tone and direction of the questioning.

'When did you find out she was married?'

'She told me about two weeks after we started seeing each other,' I said.

'By seeing each other, you mean starting sexual relations?' The junior officer pushed the tone too far.

'So, it would have been difficult to stop then,' the senior officer added as I moved from relaxed sitting to leaning forward.

'I was quite shocked when she told me, but she had said they were separated. That happened before I arrived in Fiji in late February.'

'So, you never visited her at their home?' the senior officer said.

'No, she came here several times.'

If I had started the interview under the vagueness of insobriety, it wouldn't have happened now. The police officers leaned toward each other and whispered something I didn't understand but recognised as Hindi. I'd heard Letitia speak it often during her calls home. What they said was not meant for me but was about me. Both laughed.

My phone buzzed once, then again. I ignored it and stared in disbelief at the officers sitting like two gossiping teenagers caught in their duplicity. It buzzed a third time, and I looked down at the message on the screen—it was from Kat.

'Don't say another word. Whatever you say won't help you or the police investigation. Just wait. Help is on the way.'

How did she know they were here? Then came a knock on the door I'd left open.

'Hey Jack,' said the figure standing at the doorway.

'Phil, what are you doing here? I'm kind of in the middle of something.'

'That's why I'm here,' he said.

Phil walked through the door with a confidence I hadn't seen from a man I thought was simply a house husband with a fetish for crime shows and gossip. Instead of a usual T-shirt and shorts, he wore a bright orange floral shirt, ballooning cream linen pants and brown leather sandals. He slid his hand into his pants pocket, pulled out two official business cards, and thrust them into the hands of each police officer, who looked at him in shock.

'I'm the Professor's attorney, Phil Dixon,' he announced, clarifying the uncertainty as to why he was now standing beside me and between the officers and their job. 'My client no longer wishes to answer your questions at this point. We can arrange a formal time for an interview with the Professor, but for now, I will be in attendance as my client has rights, as you know.'

'We are simply conducting a preliminary interview to clarify some points,' the senior officer protested.

'That may be so, but he has the right to be represented during such interviews, and he is now claiming that right, so the interview is over,' Phil said, exerting his authority to close the interview down. 'I need to consult with my client. At that time, we will happily answer your questions regarding Ms Singh and what has happened.'

The interview was done. The police officers stood, replaced their berets, and excused themselves. I waited a moment until they had left the apartment.

'What is going on, Phil?' I said. 'You're a lawyer?'

'All a bit of a surprise,' Phil said with a smirk. 'And I'm sorry for bouldering in like that, but trust me, you needed representation. I am offering my services, gratis, of course.'

'Ok, now all the police dramas make sense,' I said. 'Sharpening your skills.'

'Not really,' he said. 'Distractions to pass the time.'

It seemed too coincidental with the text from Kat and then Phil coming to my rescue. There was more to this than it appeared. I was unsure what that was, but it eased my anxiety and annoyance over the interview.

It took a few days, but the call came from the local police station requesting a formal interview. I redirected the call to Phil, and he made the arrangements. They agreed to the interview in a familiar and formal setting. It was scheduled at the university, and the head of school would attend. Phil and I sat down the day before the interview to plan the response to questions. He would direct any legal issues in the discussion but wanted to keep the answers clear and accurate. No elaboration.

The two interviews couldn't have been more different. From the start, the two more senior-ranking police officers were polite, introducing each other to the group that had grown by two, with the faculty secretary attending to take notes and Esther.

'We now have more information on what has happened regarding Ms Singh and her estranged husband,' the senior sergeant said. 'Can you please tell us what happened the night before the incident?'

I glanced across at Phil, and he nodded to respond. It wasn't just an approval but a reminder to be clear, concise and truthful.

'We met at the Poetry Slam at the university, where we talked with several students,' I quickly summarised. 'Letitia's husband was there but didn't interact with the group.'

'So, you never spoke to him that night?' the other senior officer said.

'Had you spoken to him previously?' the second officer asked.

'I received two threatening letters from him,' I said as the head of school handed copies to the senior sergeant. 'He texted me once asking why I was seeing his wife. I told him we would not see each other until things were sorted out, and I said he should speak with her. He didn't respond.'

'And by things, you mean their divorce,' the senior sergeant added.

'Yes,' I replied.

Phil handed a printed copy of the letters to the senior sergeant. He looked at both copies and showed them to the other officer, who read them.

'So, there were no physical interactions with her husband other than these incidents?' the senior sergeant asked.

'No,' I responded.

'When was the last time you spoke with Ms Singh?' the senior officer continued. 'Did you speak with her after the poetry event?'

'Only by text,' I said. 'I woke up and read a text Letitia sent, then went back to sleep.'

'1.14 am,' said the junior officer, handing me a printed copy of the text.

'Yes, that was the last time we communicated,' I said, placing the printout on the table next to the letters.

'We see from the texts that you'd planned to meet the following morning,' the senior sergeant said.

'Yes, Letitia was to come to the apartment at 8am.'

'The messages indicate that she wanted to leave her husband and join you.'

'Yes, that is what we'd planned. I didn't think she was safe with him, and his behaviour had become more erratic.'

'What do you mean?' the senior sergeant asked.

'More threatening,' I said, 'particularly after the incident at Letitia's home.'

Neither police officer responded to my comment. They already knew about the attempted rape.

'We believe her husband checked her phone and read the messages,' the senior officer confirmed what I had already guessed. 'We think he'd realised the marriage was over and became desperate, and we believe that's what pushed him to take her life and his own.'

It didn't make me feel any better, but it confirmed her husband was as much a coward in life as in death.

'Is that the extent of your investigation?' I said. 'You said you now knew more about what happened.'

'No, we have more information on what transpired weeks before and after she left with friends to have a few drinks downtown,' the junior officer said.

Phil asked if they could share that information, but the officers were reluctant.

'I think what we have found out might be quite confronting to you, Professor, and everyone here,' the senior officer said.

'Perhaps it's best not to discuss these details right now,' the head of school interjected.

I sensed everyone in the room knew more about the incident than I did.

'Do you know what happened?' I said to Ravi.

The officers looked at each other and started to stand up.

'Do you want to know the details?' Phil said, leaning across the chair to me.

'I think I'd rather hear the truth than gossip,' I responded.

'Well, let's get to the truth then,' Phil said to the officers.

The lower-ranked officer looked to the senior sergeant as he propped and nodded for him to sit.

'We know the husband spent many hours online planning what transpired,' the senior sergeant started without more prompting. 'We confiscated a laptop from the house, and his browser history revealed much to us. He'd meticulously researched the drug, the rope and how to make a hogtie so it wouldn't slip. We think he'd practised it, as one of the chairs in the home had rope marks and residue.'

'So, he drugged Letitia?' Phil said.

'Her friends confirmed she felt sleepy but hadn't seen her leave. Her husband was seen waiting for her outside and took her back to their house,' the senior sergeant said. 'The taxi driver said he carried her from the car to the house, saying she'd drunk too much, and he wanted to put her to bed. We have to wait for the tests, but it looks like he slipped a tranquilliser into her drink at the end of the night,' the senior police officer said.

The police found a sachet of olive-green pills, with two missing in his pants pocket. They'd tracked a conversation with a local Chinese dealer who operated out of Suva's bar street. He'd bought Rohypnol just a week earlier. If timed right, the drug would take twenty to thirty minutes to work. He'd raped her while unconscious. He'd gagged and hogtied her, unable to move. She was at his mercy. He'd learned from his first attempt to rape her.

'Didn't any of her friends notice her leaving the bar?' I asked.

'They said she'd gone when they tried to find her as the bar closed.'

'She'd stopped drinking months ago,' I added. 'Changed her life. She was proud of how much she had taken control.'

'Yes, they said she'd only been drinking water during the night,' the senior officer added.

But I could feel there was something else. Maybe it was in the way the officers gestured to each other. Or perhaps it was simply the tenseness I felt. Whatever it was, I knew there was more.

'I think we should stop there,' the senior sergeant said. 'What we found in the apartment is for the coroner to confirm and report.'

'I want to know the truth,' I protested. 'I think I deserve that.'

'I *can* say something about you,' the senior officer said.

'Me?' I responded, surprised.

'Yes, we found a detailed diary in his laptop. His thoughts and his plans for you.'

'What plans?' I said.

'He planned to kill you,' the senior officer said. 'He followed you on many occasions and wrote detailed notes about your movements, classes and times when you walked home. Did you sense anyone following you, something unusual?'

'One night, I was followed by a car, and I thought someone was at the bottom of the stairs,' I said.

'Yes, that was the first attempt,' the officer responded. 'He tried to lure you out of the apartment and into the darkness of the garden, but the neighbours scared him away.'

'And the second attempt?' I asked.

'He followed you when you were leaving campus late one evening, and you were unwell. Yes?'

'Several weeks ago, I left the class feeling dizzy. But a student passing by called a taxi.'

'That student saved your life,' the senior officer responded.

Journal

Date: 25 July 2012

What they had found wiped away any thoughts of him as inconsequential. The shadowy figure that had lurked in the background of everyone's life for so long had come into full view. He was wicked, as only the devil knew one of his disciples.

The plan of attack was meticulous, calculating as it was horrifying. I would have met the same fate as Letitia but for pure luck and happenstance.

Letitia's murder was an event of simplicity that reverberated beyond its singular act of violence. Her death was mine and mine alone. But it was utterly, sickeningly familiar. It was not another murder explained and condoned as an act of passion and jealous rage, as the media and gossipers would say. It served to do nothing more than continue a dull accepted ideological, though ill-conceived, 'truth': that men are possessive, jealous and violent and women are better served protected, isolated and restricted.

It simply helped to perpetuate a historical process that presents an inevitable, unchanging, 'natural' path, allowing the hierarchies of exploitation to continue.

Jack.

CHAPTER 26

Voices from Apted Park rolled across the thin night air. I tossed wildly, wrestling with the monstrous savagery and haunting dreams. Each roll punctuated phantasmagorical conceits playing back and forth between denial and grief. It was a universe of haunted moments like a spider's gossamer, spinning a web of implausible possibilities. The clock flipped loudly from the bedside table. Each moment passed slowly, offering unsatisfying hints of reality never to be fulfilled. As dawn drew closer, I heard a car speed up Beach Road. I wanted to spring out of bed as though there was something important to do. But the promise of another day was wiped clean—a fragile world now with little hope or reason.

The closed, rain-soaked louvres shut off any light that may have lit a path to the living room and kitchen. Underfoot, tangled, sweat-soaked clothes lay on the cold, marble floor of the living room. Knowing the apartment layout didn't help much, as I collected the side of the breakfast bar with my hip. The pain ripped through the muscle. I ignored it and grabbed a glass sitting on the sink. The first mouthful drew little satisfaction. A second wasn't enough, but any more would make me vomit. The room seemed enormous and lifeless, with the pulled curtains giving no hint of what lay outside. I stumbled across the room, feeling blindly for the light switch. My left knee clipped the edge of the coffee table, sending me careering into the guitar that strummed a high-pitched squeal. The room had a musty smell. Opening the French doors pushed the odour out the back windows.

Unbeknownst to me, others at the university were already moving to take advantage of the situation. They started to push their agenda only days after Letitia's death and before her body was returned home. Our relationship and her brutal death had become a perfect storm to realise what they saw as a desperately needed change in university leadership. They claimed it had become delinquent in protecting young women. What was required was a drastic change, and the catalyst of Letitia's death presented itself as a salacious scandal circulating the campus. To them, it screamed an opportunity to expose the leadership as contributors to this public embarrassment and kill off their enemies who had survived under the protection of the President. The moment to exploit a grieving mother they saw as the perfect foil to garner sympathy for their ambitious play at control.

Anyone who knew Letitia was invited to attend a memorial service and share their memories. Some had known her from childhood; others were colleagues from her time teaching at a high school. They spoke of how she cared for and supported them with the warmth of her charm and the comfort of her kindness. Two sizeable white cotton bed sheets lay on the floor of the Performance Centre, inviting people to write a message or draw on the canvases. Some wrote, 'I love you, Ms Letitia', while others scrawled, 'RIP Ms Leti, you will be deeply missed'. Those who knew her well drew elephants, her favourite animal. Anyone who had visited her closet-sized office couldn't help but see the row of brightly painted gold and silver animals, as many as ten or fifteen, on the bookshelf above her computer. One of those was now in my office. MummaG gifted me the small wooden carving when we packed the books in her office. I'd politely refused the offer, but she insisted.

'It's all we have left of her,' I remembered her saying as she placed another book in a box and closed the lid. I wrote *Return to Library* in large letters on the lid.

'She'd want you to have it, and I want you to have it,' she said.

I entered from the side entrance of the centre to avoid distraction. But there was no escaping the looks. Everyone knew who I was and why I was there. I glanced over and saw the seats full of people lined around the room three deep. She may have been surprised as to how many had come. I wasn't. Anyone who came into her life could not help but remember her. She had that personality, bubbly and magnetic. It drew people to her, keeping their attention through her kindness and tenderness. Letitia would be truly missed.

Sonja rose from a row of seats lining the wall to the right of the podium. Each pair of eyes followed her confident walk the short distance to the microphone. She stood comfortably behind the podium like she'd done a thousand times before. She looked out into the crowded bleachers.

Lost in my thoughts, I paid little attention to her arrival. But the growing silence turned my attention back to the podium. When we'd met, Sonja was introduced in a typical way as a graduate of such-and-such school. I never understood why people presented themselves in that way. It didn't matter what side of the Atlantic she'd honed her craft. All that mattered was the person that stood before me. One only had to spend a few minutes in her presence to recognise the charm and cleverness that made people feel important and limited in equal amounts. These qualities helped her rise above less talented. Of which there were many, and those more threatened, of which there were many more. But a sharp tongue and lack of patience for pettiness rightly or wrongly had limited her opportunities in a cut-throat world. Then came an offer from the head of school, who saw her present at a London conference. She was much more than a good speaker with a commanding grasp of her discipline. To him, she was an opportunity, a researcher of great potential, which he could capitalise upon to push his agenda at the university. She was more than happy to accommodate his pursuit.

'I see many familiar faces here today,' Sonja began slowly, trying desperately to keep her emotions in check. 'Others, I have not had the pleasure, but thank you for coming.'

Sonja paused again and took a deep breath to compose herself. There was no fear, as she'd spoken to much larger crowds. But not like this, not about this.

'I stand before you today bearing witness to Letitia's death,' she calmly stated. 'I want to testify to her life that echoed her strong feminist character and a stronger social conscience. Yet, I do not want in any way or form to retain or mention her killer. I do not want to write or speak his name, nor do I want it remembered. I find his act to be cowardice, selfishness, and pure evil. Perhaps I am guilty of not understanding the darkness and desperation of mental illnesses. What has come to bear from a difficult childhood or the system restricting men from emotional expression or seeking assistance. Perhaps Letitia's husband was an ill man who deserved my sympathy and compassion rather than my anger. Be that as it may, his act was evil, and I feel no obligation to conceal my anger and hatred of what he has taken from me, from you, from all of us.'

Sonja's eloquence was unmistakable. I could not have done what she just did. I'm unsure if anyone else could have either. I knew she was remarkable in character, but to manufacture such sturdiness in the face of her pain and loss was genuinely astounding.

Esther replaced Sonja on the dais. She'd experienced first-hand the trauma Letitia and other women faced on the islands in her consultations. One could be excused if she'd become desensitised to such horrors. But from an inner strength, Esther delivered with grace and decorum.

'Faced with such loss, people often ask why women stay. I know some were overheard whispering similar nonsensical judgements in corridors. Why had she not just left him? That question is much easier to ask than answer. I had a conversation with a male security guard, one I could not believe. He told me, honestly, that if she'd only done what she was obligated to do as a wife. It was as though she was somehow complicit in her death merely because she was a woman and had an independent spirit. Guilty on both counts, some might think. But not me or anyone who'd spoken, even for a moment, with Letitia or any other women who'd experienced such harassment and domestic trauma. It would not be betraying her confidence or memory to tell you about the horrendous pain she'd experienced at the hands of this man. No one truly knows why people stay in abusive relationships. Some do it out of love or obligation. Others out of fear of the unknown or even their life. That fear manifests from social stigma or lack of financial independence. Letitia felt both pressures. Far too often and far too many women experienced the same. Even in the face of such trauma, Letitia desperately wanted to help her husband transition to a new life without her. So, she wore the brunt of mental, emotional and manipulative abuse. Treating someone you swore to protect and love as a perverted honour killing was cowardly.'

Silence filled the auditorium. No one moved, and no one said a word. They were stunned by the honesty and truth, and only isolated sobbing filled the void where most had last seen her vibrant and happy.

Perhaps in time, Letitia's death would be considered an event of change. It must be recognised as an event that demanded society's fidelity, an act of activism that worked on rewriting the order of things. It should be recognised as a process that develops something new and universal. The evil renunciation committed by Letitia's husband must be an event that expels evil and brings good into the world.

Then, a middle-aged woman rose to her feet, hidden from my view by Letitia's parents sitting in the middle of the bottom row of seats. She paused momentarily, leaned causally into Letitia's mother, grasped her hands and whispered in her ear. It was a dramatic and seemingly unnecessary gesture. The woman then turned on her heels and strode to the podium. She rested her notes gently in front of her, standing silently for a moment before looking out into the packed bleachers.

Professor Johnstone was an odd mixture of quick parts. A middle-aged woman who exhibited intellectual qualities, abilities and talents mixed with scepticism, reserve and caprice. Her thirty years of experience had been insufficient to realise her dreams, no matter the opportunities and many places she'd tethered her questionable talents. Her character had been shaped irreversibly by that frustration. Few liked her; most feared her. Exactly what she wanted, with those in her inner circle becoming pawns in her political games. It didn't seem to matter whether they understood her character or intent. Each one was only too eager to do her bidding; each one was rewarded with position and power. For those on the outer, her intentions were less demanding to decipher. She was a woman who calculated meanness, curated information and had an uncertain temper. When discontented, mainly when things didn't go her way, she became neurotic to the point of paranoia. The business of her life was to get ahead, gain more power, and unleash her will upon those she deemed unworthy or corrupt. Her actions became more than a calling. It was a blind obsession.

'This is a tragic time,' the Deputy Vice-Chancellor of Student Affairs said, slowly raising her eyes from her notes. 'I didn't know Letitia personally, but from what I have been told, she positively impacted people's lives. We should all celebrate that, as eloquently stated by the last speakers. We heard today how she had fought for women's rights. I am also very passionate about that, and I've spent many years doing just that. And in my role, I will certainly advocate for women at the university to be afforded all the protection they need to feel safe.'

I glanced across at Ravi, sitting uncomfortably among the dignitaries to the right of the podium. He looked down and shook his head. There was no love lost there. Their running battles in the Senate had become legendary. Those clashes had become so heated at times both were asked to leave. The head of school saw the interjection as a victory over the 'ravings of a psychotic lunatic'. She saw it as males siding with one another and drowning out the voice of reason. Ravi was not just an enemy. He was an accomplice to her struggles. Then Ravi mouthed something. I couldn't quite make out what he had said. But the look on his face seemed to say this was not going anywhere positive. I looked back to the podium.

'The university takes this responsibility very seriously,' Professor Johnstone continued. 'I pledge today that my focus in the coming months will be to make this institution a safe place for young women like Letitia to study. I seek approval to implement a range of policies that ensure any form of harassment and those perpetuating it will be dealt with swiftly.'

I looked back at Ravi, who now had his face in his hands. He looked up, and the frustration was evident, and his distaste for this woman was no longer hidden. He was beyond angry. Was that a thinly veiled threat? Was she accusing me of something inappropriate, such as sexual harassment of Letitia? I'd heard the whispers of sex for grades in other schools. But that's not what happened with Letitia.

I watched the Deputy Vice-Chancellor gather her notes and walk toward the exit. As she closed in on the people blocking her path, the crowd moved quickly, allowing her to pass. To her, that parting of the ways must have seemed almost biblical. She was on a mission and woe to anyone who got in her way, including me.

Professor Johnstone's bravado and postulating might have been curtailed somewhat if she'd only waited a moment to see people interact with MummaG and her husband. Some held MummaG's hand, others briefly stopped and conveyed their feelings of loss, while others simply smiled and passed by, not knowing what to say. I waited patiently for the people to leave. MummaG leaned into her husband and whispered in his ear. She rose and walked towards me, sitting alone in the corner. I stood and stepped down the two rows of seats. She was shorter than her daughter and had the same wavy curls, though much shorter. Like Letitia, she had the kindest of eyes. She held my hands and looked up at me tenderly.

'Thank you for coming,' she said so quietly that I could barely hear her. 'So good to see you again.'

'I wasn't quite sure it would be ok for me to be here, but I had to come,' I responded. 'I couldn't stay away; it would have disrespected her and you.'

'No, you are most welcome. You are always welcome.'

The words meant far more than anything uttered in the past two hours. Here stood a woman lost in grief and fighting for a reason for that loss, and she was extending a gesture of love. We'd only met a couple of times, the first at her brother's home just days after her death. I remembered the hesitation I had felt before that meeting. I stood outside with Ravi and Sonja, waiting for Letitia's uncle to welcome us into the home. He led us to a sofa in the living room. We sat surrounded by family photos and flowers, so many memories. As the door opened from the kitchen, I looked expectantly. I remembered her face from the video at the top of the mountain as she entered the room, her eyes puffy and red. She clenched tightly to a white folded handkerchief. She desperately held onto her husband for support. She stumbled slightly as her husband helped her sit down beside me. She welcomed and thanked us politely. She could say nothing as tears tumbled down her face. Her grief broke my heart all over again. She turned and looked into my eyes. Then she did the most unexpected thing. She took my hand and squeezed it tenderly. She slowly raised her other hand to my face, lightly wiping away the tears with the handkerchief.

'She didn't deserve this,' MummaG said. 'She was a good girl, a person with a future. Why did this happen?'

'She was a special person,' I responded.

I desperately searched for something else to say to ease her pain. Nothing came.

'I wish she would not have gone back to help him,' she said, forcing out the words.

'I'm so sorry,' I said. 'I should have done more.'

'Don't blame yourself. It wasn't your fault; it was that coward. He's to blame.'

The words offered some absolution, drawing the same inner strength that Letitia had demonstrated as she fought for her independence and freedom.

CHAPTER 27

Late Saturday afternoon, Davis arrived at the apartment. I heard the sequel of the taxi's brakes, leaned over the balcony and called out to him. He looked up and waved. It was his first visit. He raised his hand, asking me to wait momentarily, and disappeared through the passenger side door to pay the driver. Davis refused the change; habits die hard. He turned and gestured with both arms outstretched like a black Christ Redeemer. The apartment had no front entrance.

'Around the back, sir,' I yelled. 'Through the garden and up the stairs to the right.'

'Ok, just a moment,' Davis responded.

Davis slipped the handle of his small travel bag over his shoulder and disappeared around the corner of the building. His urgency was not lost on me. It was only a five-minute walk from the apartment, so he could have quickly dropped his bag and walked back the short distance. It is not an unpleasant walk past rows of old colonial homes and the odd bungalow with manicured lawns and barking dogs. But he didn't like the heat, and no taxi would take a short fare if he'd headed home first. I met him atop the apartment stairs and opened the security gates. Davis stooped moderately, allowing his tall frame to safely pass under the door's arch. He didn't need to be so dramatic, except many of the doorways he'd encountered hadn't been so generous. I locked both gates as Davis dropped his bag beside the umbrella, leaning in the corner.

'Gin and tonic?' I offered.

'Yes, unless you have vodka.'

'Sorry, no. Ice? How was the trip to the resort?'

'Wonderful, it's magic over there, another world. A day or two at a resort clears the head and recharges the soul. How are you doing?'

'Other than the existential terror of looking into the abyss of loneliness and the end of a career, I think I'm doing ok. Really.'

'Sarcasm aside, you're not doing ok, are you? But I'm going to change that.'

'Really,' I said. 'It must be pretty good to drag you away from that beautiful lady and even prettier beaches on the other side.'

'It's better than good for you.'

I moved around the kitchen, organising glasses, alcohol and ice. The view from the balcony had Davis's attention.

'I wish I had this,' he said. 'You have the best view.'

'Yeah, I love this place. A view and a breeze. Beautiful at night. Pity, it's all coming to an end.'

'I've got neither, nor is it the end, I promise you. My bottom-floor apartment fronts an eight-foot concrete fence, cars passing by and people peering in. I get to wave to everyone, and that's nowhere as interesting and pleasant as this.'

'I thought you were moving to the top floor, at the far end of the building,' I said. 'You'd have a view then, not of the ocean but some greenery at the very least.'

'I missed out on that. Something about the owner's cousin or something moving in.'

'That's how it works, I've found,' I responded.

'I'd have come over sooner and more often if I'd known it was this good.'

'Well, this is a nice conversation about whatnot, but you didn't come back early to discuss the view. Something's got you excited?'

Davis didn't answer immediately. Instead, he gathered in the view some more, something he might not see again. Well, not soon enough for his liking. Maybe he was simply organising his thoughts or building more suspense for the big announcement. Either way, his lingering on the balcony started to annoy me. But since I seemed sure he would make his day, I sat on the sofa and waited. I took a long sip of my drink. Nothing on the horizon seemed like it could alter the current trajectory of events. I was still under investigation, yet no one had officially informed or contacted me. The stress of that had taken its toll. I was exhausted as every person's glance seemed tinged with suspicion and guilt.

'Look, I know she meant a lot to you,' Davis started as he encased the glass in his large mitt. 'But you need to know some things.'

'About what?'

'About Letitia and what happened with another staff member.'

I remained silent, but the look of distaste for such vagaries registered quickly on Davis.

'You know, don't you?' he said.

He guessed wrong. Well, partially.

'It doesn't matter whether I know anything or not,' I responded without a change of emotion. 'Whatever happened, it was before our time, and it doesn't matter to me what she did or didn't do or with whomever. She's dead, and that's all that matters right now.'

I'd heard the rumours. What was being said wasn't specific to Letitia. But it had washed conveniently into the talk of sex for grades. It's distasteful at best and immoral at worst. But I found gossiping about such things less than appealing, unlike others. But the breeze now dipped, and a half-sick feeling washed over me. Discovering a life apart from the one you thought you knew is discombobulating, even if you dismiss it as inconsequential. The mystery man's presence on campus was fleeting for over six weeks. No one seemed to know or care where he was, not the least the head of school. That relationship had gone south long ago when a misguided, poorly orchestrated school coup failed. Some think they are smarter than they are, and he was one of them. Any interaction between the two adversaries, short and fleeting as they were, was full of palpable contempt for anyone unlucky enough to be around them.

To be honest, I was surprised by Letitia's or anyone's interest in him. His middle-aged, rotund body suffered from the half-lazy work of a bracing personality. He knew women early, and there was a plentiful and accessible supply. Since they spoiled him, he was contemptuous of them, of young virgins, because they were both ignorant of his charm and intentions. And those with more experience, he found hysterically vulnerable of things his overwhelming self-indulgence took for granted. He collected his prey with little consideration of the vulgarness of such impulses, grooming them with hope and promise. None of this went unnoticed. People called the collective 'his girls', but no one did anything. A duty of care unfulfilled, ignored.

I'd innocently strolled into the mix, presenting an opportunity too tempting for those mindlessly fulfilling a moral obligation to protect the young and innocent. Admirable but misdirected; a rationale unfounded, misguided in this case. Nonetheless, it unleashed a series of calculated actions designed to exact maximum collateral for all deemed real or perceived threats. Such motivations went beyond protecting the young and crossed into settling old debts.

I was still unsure exactly where Davis was going with this line of questioning. He didn't engage in idle gossip. He knew it would hurt, which wasn't his style. There was always a purpose, something the friendship was founded on. But that purpose eluded me for now.

'What's the point of dragging any of this up again?' I said.

'None, but I wanted to ensure you knew what you were fighting for.'

'Fighting for, you're kidding, right? There's no fight left in me. I'm done!'

Davis glanced across at me with a look that seemed suspicious, disbelieving. He wanted a fight. It was his way, in his nature. Any injustice was a hill for him to die on. I admired that about him, but he doubted my conviction.

'I'm telling you Professor Johnstone has over-played her hand,' Davis said as he sat opposite me. 'It's time to hit back. She's weakened, exposed.'

'What do you mean?'

'The word is she's threatened the President,' Davis said quietly as though such talk might somehow be overheard. 'Accused him of complicity by knowing what was happening and not dealing with the problem. She wants him gone, as well as his position. She's setting herself up as the saviour of the university and its moral values.'

'You're kidding. If she gets control of the university, anyone not in her camp will be pushed out if they're lucky. Or professionally assassinated, starting with me.'

'You have two choices as I see it, my friend,' Davis continued. 'Fight or move on. If we play our cards right and pressure the President, we can create a situation that will play out in our favour. But be warned. There is no turning back once we start down this road. If you don't end this nonsense now, she'll keep coming after you until she gets you. And she will if you let her.'

'I have to say I've grown to love that giddy enthusiasm,' I responded with more than a tinge of sarcasm. 'However, there's a lot of ifs and hope in what you're saying. That result won't happen unless we can execute the said coup. I say that word in hushed tones here, and I believe a likely outcome will be our bloody demise.'

'That's why I'm saying we need to put pressure on the President. He's got as much if not more, to lose than you.'

'I'm going to stop you right there,' I said. 'Is your plan based on me appealing to a person I've briefly met, in a meeting I probably can't get, and saying what to him? That's not how the world works. We not only don't have any power but no access to power.'

'We don't, but Ravi does,' he responded. 'He's key to access those who now have more to lose than us. We have to make a stand, and we cannot let her get away with this.'

'I did stand, and here I am,' I said. 'I'm fighting for my professional life and a possible referral to the Integrity Committee. Even facing the committee casts a shadow over my professional integrity, which will linger forever. And the most likely outcome of that will be my dismissal.'

'You don't know that will be the result,' Davis pleaded.

'I know these people work in the shadows and have unlimited resources, and they've got a head start on me.'

'But we plead your case. Tell them the truth.'

'The truth doesn't matter, and you know it,' I responded. 'It is all about perception; I'm guilty no matter what is true. I was the person who came between a married couple.'

'That's not how it was,' Davis said.

'No, but the court of public opinion is on their side.'

'Then we have to stop this before it gets to that,' Davis responded. 'Look, I know you've got a lot on the line. Your career, your reputation. We've all lost someone important to us, her family, the community, you, and me if you leave. We can do something to take back what is good and right. You did nothing wrong professionally, and you won't even try.'

'I can't,' I responded. 'If it was anything else. I'm happy to see you and even happier you believe in me; it means everything. I've got some food in the fridge, and I can rustle up some chow if you're hungry.'

'Look, I get it. I'm happy if that is what you decide to do. Move on. But this is your second chance.'

'It won't be a second chance if I lose,' I responded. 'It will be the end of my career. If I leave, another chance will come. I can't roll the dice. I came here to save it, not to destroy it on a risky move. I've overplayed my hand before and lost badly. I can't risk that again and restart my life somewhere else, whether I did anything wrong. That's something I don't want to hang over my head. Look, if we don't talk shop, I'm happy for you to stay for dinner.'

'No dinner, but how about we get a drink? I promise no more talk of this. Let's head to the Holiday Inn, sit outside in the cool breeze and watch the sunset.'

PART FIVE

CHAPTER 28

The taxi slipped past the university campus and slowly climbed the hill. Rolling down the other side, it took a sharp left at the Y-intersection. Another hill and quick descent before taking a sharp left into a poorly lit feeder street leading to the main road. The corner's camber threw the car out onto oncoming traffic as it quickly descended into a hidden side street. There was little chance of hitting an oncoming car at this hour. The car glided down the slight incline, and the name of the road changed as it curved slightly left at the corner of the park. The road split the park into two parts, with old government buildings, a pavilion to the right, and charming, gated colonial homes to the left.

Davis and I sat on either side of the spacious Corona's large, black leather backseat. But the road was a shortcut to the foreshore and poorly maintained. As the car jolted from side to side, we slid together on the shiny, well-worn leather. The driver slowed at the T-intersection and pulled to a sharp halt. We pushed our feet against the front seats as gravity took hold. Taking a left would put us on Queen Elizabeth Drive and towards Laucala Bay and the University via the scenic beach route. But our destination lay just to the right on Victoria Parade. The car swung around the corner, and the once majestic and soon-to-be-again Grand Pacific Hotel rose against the horizon. This grand old lady, which once housed dignitaries including royals and state leaders, had crumbled at the same speed as the fledgling republic. But the iconic structure received a boost when the government stepped in and funded the rebuild after years of being a scar grotesque. The car dipped into a pothole. I looked across at Davis and saw him grip the door handle and pull himself upright.

'What's the word on the state of the hotel development?' I asked. 'Is it going to be finished on time?'

'Only know what people have been saying for years.'

'Money troubles?' I said. 'I thought that was sorted with the government purchasing it from the Nauru investors.'

'Every time work stopped, the gossip starts, and then the work begins again. I think it's more to do with weather and getting approvals than money now.'

'She'll be the majestic when everything is done. Any word on a possible opening?'

'I'm told a soft opening is planned for March next year with a full opening for May.'

'Do you think that's possible?' I asked.

'They're pretty good sources, so maybe.'

'I'm not going to ask who the source is. I can guess, though.'

'You don't want to know, and I don't want to tell you,' Davis said.

'Fair enough. Let's get a drink.'

The ride would have taken us to the bars, restaurants, curry houses and the harbour market if we'd continued along the parade. Maybe we'd venture up that way later. The taxi dipped and veered off the road into a car park, pulling up under the awning covering the hotel's entrance. We slipped from the back passenger side door and quickly hit the cold foyer air. A smiling hotel employee greeted us as we passed the concierge's desk. That soon changed as a familiar face exited from the side entrance to the manager's office and bathrooms.

'Davis,' said the approaching figure.

'Ashet,' said Davis, surprised.

I paused two steps back and waited for a hello; it never came. I nodded, but the gesture went unnoticed or simply ignored. Either way, it said more about him than me. I considered letting it die there but then reconsidered.

'Just rude,' I said, 'no surprise.'

'Easy, man,' Davis said. 'It's not worth it.'

'If I'd known he was here, I'd not bothered coming down.'

Ashet turned around and started back toward us. Davis's size was no match for the smaller man as he headed off his advance, ushering him instead toward the outside pool area. I turned and walked to the bar. I watched from the poolside dining area while Davis and Ashet talked.

Ashet appeared as a slightly larger version of a garden gnome beside Davis. Some thought of gnomes as cute and benevolent. But those people didn't know the long and sordid past of gnomes. Like fairies, gnomes are amoral creatures, capable of showing tremendous kindness one minute and unspeakable cruelty the next. The ability to slip easily and comfortably between the two made the idea of good and evil alien to them. A good psychologist would say they were archetypical narcissists. Ashet was that and some.

Given Ashet's diminutive size, the scene played out through the looking glass was almost comical. Clearly, he was listening, but he kept shaking his head each time he was asked: 'Is that what you really want?' I couldn't make out what was the 'that' he was referring to, but I knew it was about me. Ashet pulled away suddenly, revealing Davis's hand on his shoulder, which was not guiding but holding him at bay. Ashet disappeared briefly behind a group, reappearing in the doorway. His eyes fixed on me.

I turned and declined a request from the barman. There'd be no drinking tonight. As I glanced back toward the door, Davis had caught up with Ashet in mid-stride and grabbed his arm. Ashet reefed it away but stumbled and half fell into a group sitting at the table closest to the door. I wasn't afraid of Ashet. But I feared how he might react. He had been one of the most erroneous minions looking for favour from Professor Johnston. It might just be a ploy to draw me into an embarrassing confrontation. That would not help my cause right now. I opted for a quick exit through the hotel foyer. Moving past the bar area's last table and opposite the toilet corridor, I looked back, and Ashet was closing in fast. I saw Davis trying to head him off again, but he clearly couldn't stop him.

'Can't face me?' said Ashet, pointing a finger at me. 'Easier to take advantage of defenceless women.'

I sighed deeply and bit my bottom lip hard. Picking a fight with Ashet was one thing, but bringing Letitia into it was another.

'I don't need to face you,' I said, standing flush in the path of an approaching Ashet. 'I've done nothing wrong, no matter what your twisted little mind imagines. You've been drinking, so maybe you need to cool off. Go home and sleep it off.'

'Fuck you! Your days are numbered at the university. We'll make sure of that.'

'Oh, and who are we? You and some army of little handmaidens to the V-C running around inventing stories, gossiping about what you think might have happened. You can come up with whatever version you think is convenient, but that won't make a difference. I have the truth and right on my side.'

'That won't help you when we're finished with you. You're history here. And sooner than you think.'

I turned and took two steps toward the exit, but Ashet grabbed my arm, spinning me back around and sending him off balance. He then launched himself towards me but stumbled, almost falling. When he regained his balance, I was close enough to smell the alcohol on his breath. There was no avoiding him now, so either invite him outside or embarrass him. I chose the latter.

'What did you say?' I roared. 'You want me to go to the toilet and do what? I'm just not into that. But I'm sure a trip to Apted Park might work out better for you, or maybe not.'

'You seem to know it well.'

'I live right across from it. So yeah, I guess I do. I can see all matter of goings on from the second floor.'

'Really?' Ashet said.

I noticed Ashet's expression changed. That sudden realisation of his secret life was now exposed to an enemy.

'It's amazing what you can see late at night,' I continued. 'Police patrols, people getting arrested, but you know all about that, don't you?'

The look of fear now turned to humiliation and then returned to anger. Ashet wasn't expecting to be outed with his friends close by. Whatever he did to keep the story out of the press had worked, but the gossip persisted. Much of that comes from a familiar source.

Ashet moved forward and cocked his arm to take a swing at me. I didn't think I'd have to draw from previous experiences to negate such an attack. I took a step back and waited for the inevitable. But a large figure emerged from the crowd. I thought it was Davis. But he was much shorter but no less muscular. I glanced away, and a familiar face greeted me as the man gathered in Ashet with an arm locked around his chest and the other holding the swing at bay.

'How ya doin',' Jack,' said a smiling Ruben.

'My man, nice timing.'

'I've got ya back. I need that $40. Besides, I'm not sure you could take a second beating.'

It had taken some time, but Ruben had the comeback he'd indeed been waiting for to balance the one-up-man-ship ledger.

I watched as Ruben pushed a struggling Ashet toward the exit. With one hand, he opened the door of the waiting taxi and forced him into the back seat. He said something to the taxi driver and thrust twenty dollars through the window of the darkened vehicle.

'Maybe it would have been less painful for him if you clocked him one,' Davis said as he put his arm around my shoulder. 'That was brutal, but I must say deserved.'

'I know he's the Vice-Chancellor's little pawn, but that was personal,' I said.

'It's always a racial thing with him,' Davis replied.

'I get it. He's black, gay and feels persecuted,' I responded. 'The holy trinity of subjugation.'

'Interesting turn of phrase,' Davis responded. 'It's almost a cry for help with him, and I'm unsure which one applies. And that's how Ashet sees it. Every conversation with him always goes wayward. He starts wandering off into some obscure reference to a film and its meaning for *his* people.'

'Sounds like him,' I said. 'Obscurity is his stock and trade. If you can't convince, confuse.'

'Yeah, that's how he comes across sometimes,' Davis replied.

'Sometimes? You're kidding, right? All the time.'

'I think he's smart but can't put it all together meaningfully and logically. He gets lost and then starts babbling.'

'That's why he couldn't finish his doctorate,' I said. 'You need all those skills to make that possible.'

'That's another issue that plays into his pathology.'

'We'll get to that, but I am curious about what film he's referring to?' I asked.

'*The Babadook.* Do you know it?'

'You're telling me he's inspired by an obscure, low-budget Australian horror flick about a mother and son scared by an imaginary demon?'

'That's the one. Ashet interprets it as a metaphor for his gay struggle.'

'I'm so lost right now. How does that relate to Ashet being gay or gay struggle? Did he elaborate? What am I saying? Of course, he did!'

'I'm not sure I understand his reasoning, but he gave it a shot.'

'I can't wait for this.'

'We'll get to that,' Davis replied.

'So, what is the issue other than he's fucking insane?' I said.

'The real issue he has is with race,' Davis said. 'He doesn't like foreigners unless you're useful.'

'I bet that's a short list,' I said, 'but you're a foreigner, and you get along with him fine. Why is he friends with you? Why do you get a pass?'

'I'm black, and you're not.'

'Obviously,' I said. 'Lovely, the irony of being labelled by someone persecuted.'

'It's more than you as a white foreigner,' Davis continued. It comes from his childhood, traumatic as it was.'

'Isn't it always,' I replied. 'I'm wondering how that is my fault, but go on.'

'Ok, the story goes that when he was eight, his mother sent him to get some milk and bread from the local store. He wanted some candy, but his mother wouldn't give him the money for it. When the shopkeeper wasn't looking, he took a handful of candy near the checkout and stuffed them down his pants. He didn't realise there was another person in the store.'

'Argh, a foreigner.'

'That's when the situation goes pear-shaped for the little guy,' Davis said. 'He's almost out of the shop, and the customer grabs him by the scruff of the neck and hauls him back inside.'

'Did the guy rough him up?'

'I think it was more that it scared him. The foreigner told the shopkeeper about the candy, and Ashet denied it. The store owner wanted to call the police, but the foreigner, for whatever reason, pulled his shorts down and out flew the candy on the floor.'

'A little excessive.'

'That's not the end, though,' Davis continued. 'His underwear came down with the pants, so he's standing there buck naked, and several other people had walked in as the commotion unravelled, including some kids he knew. He was humiliated. Then his mother was called, dragged him home, and his father beat him senseless, as he tells it.'

'That, I'm sure, was traumatic. But let me get this straight. Ashet breaks the law by stealing and gets punished, making him hate all foreigners. Ok, not all foreigners, just the white ones.'

'He sees us as brothers-in-arms. Fighting against the injustice of racism and persecution.'

'Because you're both black.'

'Yes, but I think it goes deeper than that for him.'

'I hope so.'

'And that's where the story of *The Babadook* comes in. He honestly believes the story of terrorising a white family represents an act of queer defiance and protest. Have you seen the movie or the memes? I had to go and watch it, and it's disturbing.'

'Yes, it is as disturbing as the rationale for linking gay struggle to a horror film. I don't understand the symbolism, which is a stretch at best. Ashet does realise that most things that manifest as iconic are fabrications. And this film is no less so. It's a screenwriter's imagination.'

'Nonetheless, he believes it reflects his struggle and empowers him. He wants revenge and to gain superiority over what he called his white oppressors.'

'Well, that explains much about our interactions where he balled on endlessly to show his smartness. Most times, I had no idea what he was talking about, and I'm pretty sure he didn't either. He would launch into citing some obscure theorist and use random quotes without any explanation or relevance.'

'He does it with everyone, but you make it even more difficult for him.'

'Me, why?'

'Well, you're not just a foreigner and white, but you have a doctorate, and it was the white masters who stopped him from getting his.'

'More like his inability to string together two coherent thoughts and sentences into some semblance of an argument with evidence and rationale for whatever he was talking about.'

'Yes, but he's looking for excuses to justify his inability to get what he wants.'

'And that is?'

'Respect.'

'Don't we all?'

'Yes, and the Vice-Chancellor offers that to him, as misguided as it is.'

I didn't want to know anymore. I turned and made my way through the foyer and the exit. The doorman hailed a taxi parked at the other end of the car park, and the next car in the rank rolled slowly to a halt. The doorman opened the taxi door, and I slid into the rear seat. He looked back into the foyer, but Davis was gone. The driver paused to allow the traffic to pass, then turned right and headed toward Laucala Bay. Just before the T-intersection, he flicked the indicator to go left, like we'd driven earlier in the night. I leaned across and tapped the driver on the shoulder. If that was possible, I needed more time to process all the nonsense.

'Take the beach road, please,' I said, pointing directly ahead.

'Are you sure you want to go that way? It's longer.'

'I know, but I like the view.'

I wound the window down, and the cool ocean breeze rushed in. The driver turned and gave me a surprised look, as much to say the car was air-conditioned. I ignored the look and gazed out the window. I thought the driver would turn off the air conditioner, but he didn't. When we arrived at the apartment, I handed the driver twenty dollars and declined the change.

'Good night, sir,' said the driver and the car disappeared back toward the city and another fare.

I walked along the inner path to the apartment, climbed the stairs, and then fell into sleep—the first in seemingly forever.

CHAPTER 29

A restless night's sleep had cleared the mind and opened a path forward. I could only control what I could control, and it was time to take control. I sent an email to the Executive Director, Human Resources. It read like a request for a meeting, but the tone was more of a demand. She responded quickly, scheduling an appointment for 9.30am—no time wasting.

I arrived early at her office and spoke with the secretary at the front desk. The wait was as short as the email response.

'Thank you for meeting with me at such short notice,' I said, extending my hand to the manager.

'It seemed important,' she said, gesturing to one of two seats. 'How are you?'

Her concern seemed sincere, if not surprising. But my focus was not on her politeness.

'Let's review. I'm being investigated without being informed, accused of something I didn't do without evidence or consultation, and facing a likely disciplinary hearing for moral turpitude. I had to look that one up. It was so far out of my frame of reference and still is, by the way. I memorised it. Moral turpitude is an act or behaviour that violates the community's sentiment or accepted standard. That's a serious charge. If proven, the likely result of that charge is termination, and my career is in tatters. Did I miss anything?'

'I understand you're upset,' she said.

'Oh no, I'm beyond upset,' I responded.

'I know you feel the university has mistreated you,' she said.

'Tell me something,' I said. 'Why did you say I shouldn't resign when I mentioned it in our last meeting?'

'I really can't comment on that.'

'Ok, I will,' I said. 'I think you know this whole process, and the accusations levelled at me are complete rubbish. It's all because of an overly confident, opportunistic narcissist who thinks she's found the hobby horse to ride to the university's top position. You know what she's doing isn't right or just. That's why you said what you said. Am I wrong?'

'What has happened is out of my hands,' she responded. 'I'm not in a position to comment. I have my thoughts on it, but I'm governed by what the university wants, not what I think it should do. I'm in no position to address my concerns about the process.'

'So, you have concerns,' I said. 'You may not be able to do anything, but I can. And here's what is going to happen. I'll hire the best lawyer I can find, one that likes to take on cases like this. It won't be the best in Fiji, which you bankroll. But you're going to need him, nonetheless. Then, I will direct all my focus on taking this university apart piece by piece, individual by individual, until I have what I want.'

'I'm not sure threatening the university is the best way to go,' she responded.

'Oh, you misunderstand,' I said. 'It's not a threat, but an action with serious consequences to making the university and its hierarchy responsible for one person's hubris. I have all the time and money to do what I've said, and I will make it so uncomfortable for the university for what they have done to Letitia and me. That means I'll take this as far as possible: to the media, the Human Rights Commission and anyone else who'll listen.'

'You said you want something,' she said, redirecting the focus. 'What is it? I'll have to consult with the President.'

'I'm hoping he sees how much bad publicity and pressure will come to bear on the university and his leadership. What I want are three things. I want the investigation to cease immediately, and a full, written apology issued. I want the university to set up a scholarship in Letitia's name and fund it for three years. After that, I'll fund it personally. Imagine how that will play out in the press. And lastly, I want the Vice-Chancellor's employment terminated immediately.'

'That's a lot to ask.'

'No, it's what is fair and just. If the university and the President are unwilling or unable to comply with all the demands within 48 hours, I'll commence legal proceedings against everyone involved in this debacle. Look at my face if you don't think I'm serious.'

The discussion was over. I stood, pushed the seat back, turned, and walked slowly to the door. I glanced back to see her reach for the phone before checking whether I'd left the room. She hesitated and smiled hesitantly at me. I didn't respond as I walked out the door and toward the head of the school's office, usually a five-minute stroll away. It would take me just three minutes today. The next step was now in play. I'd enough time for a phone call to add more pressure while they were vulnerable. If this was to work, a safety net was needed. It was a last resort but a potent one. I was about to press 'end' when a soft, familiar voice answered.

'Hello, Jack,' MummaG said. 'I was just thinking of you.'

'And I of you.'

'Really, how wonderful. We haven't spoken in some time. How are you?'

'I'm sorry I haven't called. I was dealing with the university. I need your help. I'm in some trouble.'

'Trouble? Of course, anything. You're part of my family, like my son.'

Like any mother, she was protective of her flock. If circumstances were different, that's what I would have been. Her response bolstered my confidence in the plan.

'I need to tell you some things first,' I said. 'Things I haven't been completely open with you, or at least forthright. I didn't want you to worry, which I know you would.'

'It sounds serious.'

'It is,' I said, 'the university is trying to get rid of me.'

'What do you mean, fire you?'

'Yes.'

'What for? Is this to do with Letitia?'

'How did you know?'

'I had a call the other day from a person at Letitia's school. I don't remember her name.'

'Was it the Dean, the person who called?'

'Yes, a woman. She seemed rather rude, I thought.'

'What did she say?'

'She asked about you.'

'Really, what did you tell her? Please tell me everything. Don't leave anything out.'

'She asked whether you had contacted the family or me since Letitia passed. She asked what I thought of you. Did I think you were a good person? To be honest, I got very mad at her. I asked why she was asking me such questions about you. I told her straight that you'd been good to us, to me. You'd called, asking how I was and if you could do anything. I told her that she shouldn't be asking such questions and that you were my friend, and she should leave us alone, leave you alone. Allow us to grieve. Does this call have something to do with what's happening with your job?'

'I think it might,' I responded. 'Look, here's what's happening. Some in the university say I used my position to force Letitia into being with me.'

'That's ridiculous,' MummaG responded. 'She loved you, and you loved her. Who do these people think they are? Tell me who I need to talk to. I'll tell them what for.'

'That's the thing, no one from the university has bothered to talk with me. To find out what happened. The woman pushing this has just decided I'm evil, used my position to break up the marriage, and I needed to be punished.'

'Who is this woman?'

'You've met her,' I said. 'She was the one who made that speech as Letitia's memorial service and sat beside you.'

'Oh, her. I didn't like her,' MummaG said. 'She made me feel uncomfortable.'

'She has that way with people, kind of grating, irritating.'

'Yes, she didn't seem honest, like she cared for Letitia or us.'

'She thinks I am at fault. That was directed at me when she said the people who would pay for what happened.

'You didn't do that at all. Their marriage was over before you arrived. Why would she say such things, tell such lies?'

'It's a long story. The professor thinks she's doing the right thing but to the wrong person.'

'I see,' MummaG said. 'What can I do?'

'I need to ask a big favour. You can say no if you don't feel comfortable doing it. Ok?'

'Ok, but I want to help if I can. You are very special to us, to me.'

'I've told the university I won't stand and let them ruin Letitia's reputation nor mine. I want a formal meeting with the President, and I'll tell him exactly what I told the Human Resources person. I have all the time and money to fight the university. I won't stop until they end the investigation, apologise, and fire the woman making the accusations against me. If I play my hand right, I can get them to do the first two, but the last one is an outside chance. Can you help me?'

'Of course. Anything. What do you want me to do?

'Would you talk to the President if I call you?

'I'll call him now,' MummaG growled into the phone.

'Not yet,' I said. 'It may not come to that. If it does, can I count on you to take a call from the President and tell him what you think about all of this?'

'Yes, give him my number, and I'll tell him exactly what I think. I don't like people calling me asking about you, and they should not do that to you. It was that bastard of a husband, and he's at fault, and he's the coward that did this and no one else.'

The call had taken longer than expected. I'd stood as far away from the stairs so no one would hear the conversation. I'd almost done everything I could, and now it was up to Ravi to get the meeting with the President. I wasn't sure he could pull that off. But if half of the stories he told about his friendship with the President were true, then there was a chance he could leverage a meeting. I knocked on his office door, but no answer. I knocked again, and then a voice echoed down the corridor.

'I'm not in,' Ravi said.

'Well, now you are,' I replied. 'I need five minutes with you.'

'I'm actually about to go into a meeting, and I just popped back to grab a file I'd forgotten.'

'Now you'll be late. I need five minutes.'

'Sounds important.'

We sat down, and he turned on his computer. But I wasn't about to be fobbed off.

'You don't need your computer for this, and we've got five minutes, so let's get to it.'

'I'm not sure I like that tone,' he said.

'Like it or not, I'd pay close attention if you want your nemesis gone.'

'I'm listening.'

'I want you to call the President and schedule a meeting today.'

'Why the urgency?'

'I just spoke with Human Resources and threatened the university with legal action, and I will follow through. If he doesn't want a shitload of bad publicity, he needs to meet with me now, and I need you if you're up for it.'

'It seems like you're running the show now.'

'When it comes to this, yes!'

'About time,' Ravi replied. 'That's the person I want running this school. What do you want me to say?'

Ravi picked up the phone and dialled the four-digit, quick-connect number. The secretary tried to stall for several minutes, then returned to the line. He pressed the speaker button so that I could hear her.

'Tell him I need to speak to him urgently,' Ravi said curtly.

'He's quite busy today and much of tomorrow,' the woman replied. 'Maybe I can schedule an appointment for later in the week.'

'That will be too late, I think. Tell the President he needs to take this call in his best interests and the university.'

'What is about?'

'I'd like to discuss that with him,' Ravi responded.

'He won't take the call if he doesn't know what you want.'

'Ok, the university is about to land on the front page of the newspapers, and it will be about facing legal action over negligence, unfair dismissal and claims of human rights abuse,' Ravi replied. 'Of course, if the President wants that kind of bad publicity as he comes up for reappointment next month, then don't take the meeting.'

'Wait a moment,' she responded.

That moment went on for exactly thirty seconds. I went to say something, but Ravi held his index finger to his lips and pointed at the receiver and then his ear.

'You never know who is listening,' he mouthed.

The secretary came back on the line.

'He'll call you back in five minutes,' she said.

'I hope so because I have a furious and determined employee sitting here, and he's not going to take no for an answer, I can tell you that. All this craziness about an investigation might unravel very quickly and publicly.'

Ravi put down the phone and paused for a second. I thought about what might be happening at the other end.

'I guarantee you he's making two calls,' said Ravi, anticipating my response. 'The first one is to the Human Resource people.'

'And the second?'

'To the university lawyers to see where they stand.'

'Good,' I said. 'They'll need to make that last call if the university wants this to disappear.'

'You seem pretty confident it will.'

'Not at all,' I lied. 'But I'm determined to save Letitia's reputation and my career. I have good advice that he's under a lot of pressure and that they are exposed legally. So, I am hopeful he's concerned enough about his tenure at the university to pressure him to act.'

Ravi looked at me in a way I hadn't seen before. It was the look of a child who lied, and he knew it. For the first time, I knew more than him.

'What happened with Human Resources?' Ravi asked. 'What did you say?'

I gave him the short version, as much as he needed to know.

'It wasn't a conversation but an ultimatum,' Ravi responded. 'She's a smart operator and would have called the President or lawyers. Either way, they know what's coming.'

I didn't mention Letitia's mother, as he would have advised me not to bring her into this like he'd advised me not to attend the funeral. I didn't listen then, and I wouldn't listen now. She wouldn't be part of this unless it were necessary.

The call came. It wasn't five minutes, maybe three at most. I hoped the speed of the response reflected the elevated concern of the President. He hung up the phone and smiled.

'You've got your meeting,' Ravi said. 'Now, what are you going to say to him?'

'Are you coming with me?' I said, ignoring his question.

'Absolutely, I'm not going to miss this.'

'You'll know in a moment. When is the meeting?'

'Now.'

'Good, we've got them by the balls. I'm going to squeeze until I get what I want.'

'That is?'

'Stop the investigation, officially clear me of wrongdoing, and protect Letitia's image.'

'What else.'

'I want her fired.'

'I doubt you'll get that.'

'If I don't, this is all for nothing because she'll keep coming after me until she gets what she wants. Me!'

'This is going to be fun,' Ravi said in an uncomfortable tone.

Ravi's look was one of pure joy. That bloodthirsty trait didn't sit well with me, but we had a common interest now and aligned objectives. But like him, I knew what had to be done would have a lasting impact on everyone if it didn't work.

I felt a little excited, or maybe it was adrenaline. I'd had a glimpse into a world where the kill was as exhilarating as the hunt. Her world. Ravi's world. Now, my world, if only for one last desperate bid to save myself and Letitia's legacy. We walked past the coffee shop and up a slight incline to the President's office. The same voice on the telephone greeted us politely and asked us to take a seat.

'He'll be a minute,' she said.

She picked up the phone and announced we'd arrived.

'Come in, Dr Graham,' the President said, nodding at Ravi and pointing us to a small leather lounge fronting a small round coffee table. 'It has been a while since we spoke.'

'I think we should have spoken sooner than now about the investigation,' I responded. 'One I was only unaware of a few days ago. Honestly, I'm still confused about why I am being investigated.'

'I can't speak to the investigation as it has not yet been completed.'

'That's why I'm here to discuss why I am being investigated,' I responded. 'I understand that Professor Johnstone is accusing me of moral turpitude, though I'm unaware of the exact charge as no one from the university has spoken with me to hear my side of the story.'

'Please tell me what happened from the start,' the President said.

I locked into the details without focusing on anything personal. I explained how we'd met and the situation of Letitia's marriage, and I'd reported the relationship to the head of school as required by the university. I took a deep breath but couldn't control my emotions anymore. I hadn't spoken of her death in almost two months, but it was with me daily.

'I see,' said the President, handing me a tissue from the box on the coffee table. 'I understand that Letitia meant a lot to you.'

'With due respect, I loved her, and she loved me. And to be accused of manipulating her is an insult to Letitia. If this investigation goes ahead and I face a university disciplinary committee, my career and Letitia's reputation will be ruined.'

'We have policies and procedures to follow, and one of those is to investigate such claims and decide based on evidence.'

'Evidence of what?'

'Of any wrongdoing by staff in the case of a student.'

'I think that's the point, Mr President, we're trying make,' said Ravi. 'He's saying this was not a relationship between a staff member and a student, but between two mature, consenting adults who are both university staff members.'

'That's what we are trying to determine,' the President responded. 'Whether Dr Graham has behaved in a way that transgressed professional standards of behaviour.'

'Is this the kind of professional behaviour where a staff member calls the mother of a deceased person and asks her opinion about whether I am a good person? Is that kind of behaviour appropriate?'

'I wasn't aware that anyone had called Letitia's mother.'

'Then perhaps you'd like to speak to her yourself,' I said. 'She is distraught over the phone call and why you are asking questions about me.'

'You have spoken with her.'

'We speak almost every day, and I called her this morning. She wants to talk with you, and I have her number on my phone. Would you like me to call her?'

I didn't wait for a response and made the call. It rang once, then again, and MummaG answered.

'Hello, Jack,' she said. 'Is the President there? I'd like to speak with him, please.'

'He's sitting opposite me,' I said, handing the phone to the President.

I wasn't sure what she was saying, but it wasn't going well for the President by the look on his face. I glanced across at Ravi, who could hear and understand MummaG. He casually looked away, and I caught the remanence of a wry smile. I couldn't wait to ask what she had told him. But that would come later. The conversation lasted just a few minutes, and the President handed the phone to me.

'Ok, that makes it much clearer about what has been going on,' the President said. 'I was unaware of much of this. You didn't just come here to tell me this or for me to speak to Letitia's mother. What do you want?'

'I'm sure you've spoken to Human Resources, and the answer to both our problems is simple. Stop the investigation, apologise, and deal with the person who has stepped over the line with this investigation.'

'I'm not sure we can do that.'

'Ok, then I will start legal proceedings immediately,' I responded. 'I have spoken to a lawyer,' I lied. 'Maybe you already have too. I have good advice that your Vice-Chancellor has put the university in a legally exposed situation. It's up to you. I'm moving forward unless these three points are met. You have much to consider, so I'll let you decide whether you want to face a publicity nightmare. Thank you for your time.'

Ravi and I stood up and walked toward the door. But before we reached the hallway, the President called Ravi back into his office. He looked at me and nodded a reassurance. I walked into the corridor, and the door closed behind me. Inside, both men talk for ten minutes.

'What did he want to talk about?' I asked as Ravi joined me in the corridor.

'I think he's weighing up what might happen now. He was shocked by the conversation with Letitia's mother. You surprised me too when you called her; I wasn't expecting that. Nicely played.'

'There is nothing more powerful than a mother's love,' I responded.

'I understand she wanted to protect Letitia, but I'm surprised she was so angry about how the university treated you.'

'What did she say?'

'She told him she was appalled how someone had called her and that they seemed to doubt your intentions. She put him straight and even swore at him once or twice. She was furious.'

'That comes from the heart,' I responded. 'We've become close over the last two months, and that bond will never be broken.'

'I didn't realise you had been in contact with her so much.'

'As I said, we've spoken almost every day. I wanted to be there for her, and she's not about to lose a daughter and a son.'

'Yes, that's what she called you, her son. I think that had the biggest impact on the President. He now realises how the university would look if the mother of a murdered woman got up and supported the person the university blamed.'

'Exactly,' I said. 'She would do that in a heartbeat to protect me, and it would be a nightmare publicly for the university.'

'Agree,' Ravi said. 'I told him not to take too long if he wanted to make this all disappear.'

'I guess we'll just have to wait and see what happens.'

Rain clouds formed over the campus as we arrived at the school building. I hoped it was a good sign. I'd done all I could so either the university would decide or I would. At least it was clear now of the consequences. I grabbed an umbrella from my office and passed the security gates when a text came. I removed the phone from my pocket and looked at the sender.

'*We need to talk. Call me.*'

Kat seemed to know things before anyone else. I didn't care how she knew; she was on my side.

'That certainly raised the temperature,' she said.

'It was a big play, but to be honest, I was pretty desperate,' I responded.

'Desperate or not, I think it worked. I overheard a phone call between my father and his brother from the study at home, which was interesting.'

'That's heartening,' I said.

'Nothing definite, but you've scared them, and that's a good thing.'

'Thanks for the call,' I said. 'I appreciate everything you've done.'

'The least I could do,' Kat responded. 'You've been kind and supportive of me. Maybe a little judgmental at times, but we both land where the importance of truth and fairness matters. Rest, doctor, you've earned a break.'

I wasn't sure what kind of break she meant, but I'd take both right now.

CHAPTER 30

The smaller of the two big islands is less than an hour by air. A long, narrow swathe of land hugged by a rugged mountain range splits the island. The mountains cast a soft grey-blue haze on the ridges and furrows along the windward southern coasts, making them much wetter. To the north, the valley was dry most of the year, with sugar cane fields stretching out across the foothills. It attracted farmers to the fertile soils, almost like climbing into the lap of a beloved mother. A three-river delta wound through the valleys and emptied into Macuata Bay. Large vessels with cargo ships dropping anchor in the newly built port facility could not navigate these rivers.

Within the valley, colourful, simple wooden box houses dotted the fields, each with clothes drying on makeshift lines stretching out towards the sun. A palate of turquoise green, ocean blues, sun orange and pink rose houses appeared randomly along Cross Island Road. Each house was a small oasis, shaded by palm trees, a retreat from the relenting heat of the midday sun. Train tracks ran parallel to the road, back to the sugar cane mill. The sweet smell of crushed sugar wafted across the adjoining fields and through the open window of the taxi. It reminded me of my childhood and home. The cane-cutting season ran from July to December most years, and I remembered the blackness of hands sweet with that burnt smell.

MummaG stood alone at the top of the rise leading to the house. She welcomed me with a hug. Instead of taking me into the house, she led me across low grass to the large, familiar, overhanging mango tree at the property's front edge. Just a few metres away, the ground gave way suddenly, falling fifty metres to the road below. The heat seared against my shoulders, and the sweat dripped down my cheek and beard. No exaggerations were needed when people said the heat was like no other island. Some even compared Labasa to the sun, but they'd gladly live on the sun and rent out the island. The thick cover of the tree's canopy gave instant relief. It may have only dropped the temperature by a degree or two, but the cool breeze from the bay gave the illusion of comfort.

I stood next to a rickety old table made of packing palette wood as MummaG retreated to the house. Splinters from the old pine ran along the side of the wooden lengths. Nails hooked right and left were not flush with the wood. It was as if no attention was paid to fortifying the longevity of the design. The table swayed among the ankle-length grass, creaking with the breeze, unsure whether to give up or bend to its will. I reached out to test its strength and pushed it lightly to one side. It sprung back like an elastic band, coming to rest but not in its original position. I looked at the two chairs on opposite sides of the table and chose the one that looked sturdier. But looks can be deceiving as the chair creaked its disapproval when I leaned back against the wooden frame. I placed the large box I'd carried on the flight next to me on the ground, unsure the table would support its weight.

'The house is much too hot now,' MummaG said. 'We sit out here most of the day.'

'I see why; the breeze makes it quite comfortable,' I replied.

MummaG balanced two glasses and the pitcher of freshly squeezed lemon juice. She placed them carefully on the table, and it swayed slightly. I put my hand on the edge just in case it gave way, which I was sure it might do at any moment. But it stood firm. I remained convinced its days were numbered, but not today. I poured the almost clear juice into the glasses, and we sipped the coolness. Though watered down, its tartness remained with only a whisper of its former potency. But its coolness offered another layer of relief from the heat, trying its best to seep through and under the shaded dome.

MummaG left and returned with two silver bowls, one empty and the other overflowing with pinkish roots, much like ginger. She placed the empty bowl on the table as I nervously assessed how much weight it could take. But I was much more curious about what was in the other bowl. She sat on the chair and placed the bowl on her lap, resting comfortably in the sling of her maroon-coloured sari and splayed legs. She took one of the roots from the bowl and a small knife. She sliced the ends of the root, revealing a yellow interior that shone with an unearthly radiance. The outer skin was stripped away with surgical diligence, tossing the now exposed root into the second bowl on the table.

'What's in the bowl,' I asked.

'Turmeric root,' she said with a hint of surprise. 'You've not seen this before?'

'No,' I said. 'I know of Turmeric, and I've seen it in powdered form.'

'I take off the skin, soak it and then make it into a paste. It is stronger, better for cooking curries, and has a nicer flavour.'

'Will that make a lot of paste?'

'I hope so,' she said. 'I sell it to the vendors at the market. Some extra money for us.'

I didn't know how much paste the bowl of Turmeric would make, but it didn't seem enough to make money from selling it at the markets. But it was only the base used to make the paste. Adding cinnamon, black pepper, ginger, and coconut oil made the base paste a formidable mix, transferring its bitterness into the signature yellowness.

'We'll use some of it for the goat curry I'll cook for you tonight,' she said, pointing off into the distance.

Letitia's father stood next to a sizeable forty-four-gallon drum that had once contained oil, petrol or some other liquid. It wasn't clear from the decayed signage on the side. The noise from passing cars on the main road below the property hid his arrival. But whatever he had brought with him immediately attracted the attention of the two emaciated dogs that had emerged from under the house. The breed was not evident as they looked more like strays than family pets. No one paid much attention to keeping bloodlines or spading animals on the islands. What proliferated were wild animals that gravitated to wherever leftover scraps were plentiful. Today, they hoped to scavenge a few pickings, some from the freshly killed goat that lay prone on the drum. They might secure a few morsels of meat at best as the cleaver slashed into the flesh and bone. At worst, they'd get some of the unwanted offal that fell to the ground below as each blow dismembered the carcass. But that would be lean pickings, too, with most of the animal's organs cooked up for meals. Nothing was wasted, especially when money was in short supply. It was enough for the dogs to sacrifice the coolness of the house and weather the hot sun in the hope their luck might change. Each blow lured them closer to the drum as they inched toward the wafting temptation so precariously in reach.

'I've eaten goat curry only once before,' I said. 'In Tanzania when a Kenyan friend dragged me around Dar es Salaam for most of a day to find the best curry.'

'Did you like it?' MummaG asked.

'It was good, quite spicy, which I like.'

'Mine's not so spicy, but the Turmeric will make it taste nice. I hope you'll like it.'

'I'm sure I will,' I said. 'Letitia said you were the best cook.'

'Did she?' MummaG said.

It was the first time either of us had mentioned her name. Two months had passed, and rawness remained. My loss was hard enough, but that was nothing compared to the loss of a child, no matter the age. Can a parent ever move past that?

'Can I ask a question, something I've wanted to know for some time?' I said.

'Of course, anything,' she replied.

'That day you spoke to the President, what did you say to him?'

'I scolded him with my words,' she said. 'I told him it's all lies. They should have said something when we went across to bring Letitia's body home.'

'Did you meet with them?'

'Yes, just a short meeting with the President and a woman, Vice-Chancellor something or other. I can't remember her name, but not the same one who spoke that day at Letitia's vigil.'

'The other woman's no longer with the university,' I said. 'They fired her the day after you spoke to the President.'

'Good, I didn't like her at all,' MummaG admitted. 'Her words were not sincere, I don't think. I can tell when people mean what they say, and she wasn't saying anything I wanted to hear. When they started blaming you for what happened to my beautiful Letitia, I told them it was not true. Where were they when we went to get our daughter's stuff? Only you helped us bring cartons and other things to the office and house.'

I remembered that day we gathered Letitia's belongings as though it were yesterday. MummaG only took a few personal things from the office. After that, we'd headed to Letitia's house to sort through her items, some clothes and jewellery. I looked for the library books the university had asked to be returned. Just being in the house where she'd been killed was heartbreaking. Within minutes of arriving, a car pulled into the backyard and outpoured four people I didn't know. But MummaG knew them. They'd heard MummaG and a foreigner were at the house, and they'd come to secure their precious inheritance. Each book and item placed in a box was removed and scoured over to see if it was something they wanted or could sell. Vultures at the ready to take whatever would earn them a dollar.

'What you said to the President worked,' I said.

'I told him I don't want to hear anything about you. So, everyone better be quiet about that.'

Inside MummaG's house, plates, boxes and cooking utensils were piled on a large table separating the kitchen from the living area. I placed the box containing the food processor. It was something Letitia would have willingly bought for her. Then, something caught my attention. As I neared the corner of the room, I felt a hand on my arm. Maybe it was to guide me or simply support her heartbreak. A candle flickered with the light breeze from the open window. She reached out and picked up the smaller of the two framed photographs. Letitia's broad smile drew my attention. It was her wedding. Beautiful, gold and silver encrusted scarf lay over her hair with an ornate, shell-like ornament dangling delicately down onto her forehead. A fire-engine red sari wrapped around her shoulders, laden with a red, white and yellow floral lay. Her eyes were alive with the moment—happy, peaceful, content. The second photo was of Letitia and her husband sitting together, surrounded by family. He sat next to his bride, dressed in a cream suit and the same-coloured lays draped around his neck.

'They both look very happy,' I said.

'Letitia was so happy that day,' MummaG replied. 'It was what she wanted, to be with him and make a family. It was a beautiful wedding with friends and family from all over. I was so proud of her. But I was worried the photos might make you unhappy.'

'No, I wanted her to be happy above all else,' I said. 'I just wanted to help her get back to that.'

'She said you made her the happiest she'd ever been,' MummaG said. 'You and her together was what she looked forward to when she left here. That bastard took all that away from her, you and me.'

I felt her hand slip from my arm, and she melted into the sofa and sobbed. She didn't want to remember the pain, but it was as raw as it had ever been—she felt it every minute of every day. No matter what I did, that would be the way it was. I knelt next to her and held her hand. She looked up, and tears filled her eyes with overwhelming loss. Life would never be the same for her or anyone close to Letitia. That was true no matter what I did to soften the pain. I felt it, too, but losing someone from such the selfish act of a jealous, petty man she'd entrusted to care for her daughter was more than anyone could bear.

Overnight, the rain tumbled down, subduing the heat. But as the morning moved on, it would inevitably return. I heard a mix of songs and wailing from across the valley. Each is different but does much the same thing in praising a god. These were other beliefs that were essentially the same thing. I was not religious, but I understood and appreciated faith from the time spent with people who rested their existence on something more than flesh and bone. Each one captured the truth and tragedy of what lay before me. This world had wholly and utterly fallen. It spares no one and extends to every part of one's life, but I knew, too, that time had tempered the coward's offence. I needed to respond with compassion and love and learn from the tragic experience. That would allow me to move forward with an appreciation for what had been and might have become. Part of that was to respect those who shaped my life for the good and the bad. I needed to do one more thing, and my journey of redemption would end.

The taxi swept along the Cross Island Road. I looked out at the half-lowered window, and my thoughts wandered to happier times. That ended when the taxi stopped outside a gated road that led to the old wooden structure some fifty metres away.

'Just walk through the gate,' the driver said. 'It'll be ok; there's no one around.'

'Thank you. I'll be there in a few minutes, and then we can head to the airport,' I replied.

The driver nodded and waited for me as I walked along the muddied road to the funeral pyre where I'd watched Letitia's body, clad in her yellow wedding dress, be consumed by fire. I looked up to the hill where the women had sung hymns loud enough to be heard above the sound of men talking and the fire that sent Letitia's ashes skyward. There were no protests, but maybe some good had come from such a profound loss.

CHAPTER 31

The sudden jolt of the plane dropping down through the low-lying clouds over the bay brings a vulnerability to travelling in the archipelago. It takes only an hour at most, but its shortness of flight is easily matched by the robustness of its arc between the two islands. There's nothing like flying in a twin-prop ATR42-600 as it bumps and weaves through turbulence. As the plane breaks through the whiteness to the lush, green expanse below, you feel a rush of relief as it aligns its approach into the quaintly labelled international airport.

Today, it only caters for inter-island transits. I wondered how it accommodated international flights with the runway matching the briefness of the steel baggage carousel that creaked and moaned under the weight of ten bags at a time. Watching the airport staff wait patiently for the passengers to take a bag was slightly more entertaining than watching people jostle for a taxi to take a forty-minute ride to the city. It always seemed strange that the drive to town took almost as long as it did for the flight.

I was in no rush, so I stood back from the push and shove of the passengers vying for a ride. The promotion meeting wasn't for a few hours, giving me time to drop off my bags and shower before heading to campus. Whatever their decision, I had stayed true to the path. I had gotten what I demanded, and that was far more important. But the promotion was deserved.

Much of the taxi ride was as mundane as the attempted conversation with the driver. I listened, nodded and asked a few questions. Then, the radio caught my attention. The driver had turned the volume to almost a whisper, but I could still hear the song.

'Can you turn the volume up?' I asked.

'You know this song, it's one of my favourites,' the driver said.

'Mine too, mine too.'

It seemed almost prophetic as Marley swooned not to worry about a thing. Maybe today's meeting would make every little thing alright.

I arrived at the school's boardroom fifteen minutes before the scheduled meeting at 2pm. That would have seemed ridiculous, given the lack of urgency for an organised event, but this was different, and I wanted it done. So did the staff, as colleagues and invited university management, shuffled into the room on time. I scanned the room. Places for twelve good and true jury members would decide my fate. How appropriate. But the thirteenth seat was empty at the end of the table. Was that the casting vote? I had known a week before who was on the 12-member panel. But why the vacant seat?

Ravi invited me to sit next to him. The large wooden table had a ten-centimetre-high manilla folder in front of each panel member. Contained within these folders was the accumulation of an academic career spanning almost twenty years. What lay outside of that lineage of experience and publishing was the gossip and innuendo now attached to me. It seemed unfair that these could wipe away all the good I'd done and achieved. I hoped these people could see past that or at least understand the deception and deceit that had transpired and look only at what lay before them and the future I could deliver for the university.

Each member opened the files and dutifully scanned the documents. The boardroom door opened, and middle-aged women entered and moved quickly to the empty seat at the opposite end of the table. Deputy Vice-Chancellor Peters wore a formal blue business suit with a pressed white shirt. She had an air of confidence that transcended the casualness of all others at the meeting. The group fell silent as she nodded to Ravi to get underway. There was no introduction, no exchange of pleasantries. It was all business, and I wouldn't have it any other way. After all, there were other things to focus on, and I wanted to move on either way. I hadn't officially met the Vice-Chancellor for Academic Staff, but I knew of her reputation. She was not someone to be trifled with. That earned her respect. At least, I would get a fair hearing from the person who'd become the internal architect of Professor Johnstone's demise.

'Let's begin with the guidelines and process for this promotional meeting,' said the head of school, who was now standing. A quick overview and questions for Dr Graham, then we will convene separately and decide. Let's keep this meeting to forty-five minutes, so keep your questions and comments focused on the task.'

I was surprised by the proposed shortness of the meeting, which was a good sign. There were no extended questions, discussions, or deliberations. The guidelines that asked the members to stay on-task made me feel more comfortable. Some questions required simple responses to confirm what was already laid in the document they should have read. Some, of course, had not. Other questions were more focused on the future, and that's what I wanted people to think about. No one broached the elephant in the room, which perfectly suited me.

'I have a question,' said an older professor, raising his hand as though at grade school. 'I understand that you will be taking over the head of school role soon, so how do you see the school developing a more international program of study?'

'What the head of school has accomplished has been significant, and I congratulate him on his vision and hard work,' I said diplomatically. 'He's strengthened the teaching staff with crucial appointments and lifted the research standards, resulting in the school now leading the university in publishing and research impact. That is something I want to build on. I see opportunities to gain more international accreditation for our programs of study with a review of the courses and continual refinement in line with quality assurance guidelines the university and the school have adopted. I have had many curricula design experiences in the United States, China, and the Middle East.'

'How do you see the school expanding its offerings to our satellite campuses throughout the region?' another colleague asked.

'I have been working on developing digital courses that can be delivered in multi-mode learning,' I replied. 'We recognise the considerable challenges students face at the satellite campuses, particularly access to high-speed internet. Over the last couple of months, several communication and literature courses have been developed in this mode, and we have received positive responses from the quality assurance assessors in Australia. We need to refine some aspects to meet important pedagogical concerns in scaffolding and content, assessment, and activity alignment to learning outcomes, but these do not pose a significant challenge. When refined and approved, we can use these as models to process other priority courses in this learning mode.'

Other panel members remained silent, either content with the material in front of them and the responses or unwilling or able to process a question that would advance the assessment focus without embarrassing themselves. Either way, no one wanted to venture any further with questions. But I wasn't convinced the meeting was over just yet, and the shuffle of papers and chair movement at the far end of the table confirmed what I anticipated.

'I just have one question for you,' Professor Peters interrupted. 'Given how we have treated you, why would you want to work here?'

'That's an excellent question and not an easy answer,' I replied. 'I have to say that what has transpired over the past six months made me doubt why I would want to stay at the university. But I have unfinished business here. If you give me the opportunity, I'll build on the strength of the current program that the university would be proud of internationally. It also gives me a chance to make sure all that has happened, all that we have lost, is not forgotten.'

I expelled a gentle sigh that brushed my lips as though exhaling for the last time might somehow diminish its chaos. The weariness of the past six months weighed heavily. But it wasn't a sigh of frustration but one of resolution. I gathered the documents from the tabletop and excused myself for the committee to convene.

CHAPTER 32

The committee's response came swiftly. A short deliberation from the jury would usually mean a guilty verdict. I opened the email, and the smile wasn't one of happiness. It was vindication. I closed my eyes, and my thoughts wandered back.

Everything ends. But sometimes, that ending is not how you foresaw things playing out. But that's life. It's the harsh reality of the people we meet and fall in love with and what transpires from that. There is no rhyme or reason for things. These are just the moments. Some of them are harsh, unrelenting lessons. Others are wondrous and magical. Some are both. No matter which ones become your fate, there is always something to learn from the life we are dealt. Sometimes, it takes some searching.

A knock at the office door pulled my attention away. A familiar face appeared through the glass frame. The woman smiled and gestured to see if she could come in. I nodded, and the door opened. She handed me a brown envelope.

'I wanted to deliver this personally,' the Executive Director of Human Resources said.

I thanked her as she left the room and walked past the computers. I didn't follow her exit as I removed the folded white one-page letter and opened it—an official response to the investigation.

Dr. Jack Graham
Professor, Creative Writing Program
The School of Law, Arts & Media

Dear Dr Graham,

This letter officially acknowledges that the complaint lodged against you regarding your relationship with Ms Singh was dealt with as required under the various management and governance protocols. The complaint was deemed invalid to warrant official investigation under the University's conduct policy.

On behalf of the University, I appreciate the patience and cooperation you provided to me and others in the difficult discussions arising from this complaint.\

I wish you the best and continued success at the University.

Sincerely,

Executive Director, Human Resources

I slowly eased back, comforted by the chair's cushioned seat and thoughts of the two journeys. One was filled with danger, death and despair. The other with adventure, wonder and love. No one could have known how these two worlds would collide. No one could understand how cruel and uncaring the world could be. It is a world that doesn't care if you live or die, and it won't listen to your wails of despair and loss. It doesn't care about your mortality. I told myself that when I meet God, I would ask: How can you make a world with such beauty, wonder and love and fill it with such monsters? Why make flowers bloom but allow serpents to lie in wait? What purpose does the light serve if you don't let it shine? I knew the answer. God didn't make the world for us to survive; we only had to endure.

Journal

Date: 3 September 2012

Death surrounds us all. It follows us like a vagrant dog searching for morsels of food, ready to devour whatever is found without hesitation or consideration, much like the pain of loss that consumes me.

It is impossible to understand how it benefits humanity, yet it shows no remorse, no restraint. Pain only reminds us of what could have been, and the lessons learned from our experiences.

It is much easier to understand passion, love and desire; each nurtures the soul, giving the world meaning and clarity. But grief baffles me. People say the pain fades, and the good memories return, casting an eternal light upon the once desolate, forsaken landscape. That may be true. One day, I would die, along with my shattered heart.

But not today!

Jack

THE END

PART SIX

BIOGRAPHY

Ian Weber is an Australian futures thinker, writer, and researcher on gender equality activism and advocacy. As a male-feminist, he "speaks out" on issues of gender violence, stalking, harassment, and partner femicide. Ian completed a PhD in creative writing PhD titled *Autocorrect: Writing Autobiografiction as Radical Transformative Practice on Gendered Violence and Social Justice* in 2025. This practice-led research focuses on the novel *Apted Park* as lived experience and literary theory—equal parts memoir and manifesto. From *Apted Park*'s volatile love triangle to the layered exegesis, this is more than an autobiography—it's a narrative revolution that carries an intellectual torch, igniting a mission to end violence against women and children by amplifying the reach and resonance of its evidence-informed work.